LOVE WAS NOT BLIND ENOUGH

The captivating Henry Linton urged Consuela to elope with him. It seemed a most irresistible offer, for she would then possess not only this young man who was all she could want in a husband, but also the title to which he was heir.

The infuriating, loathsome Captain Nicholas Bannion insisted that Consuela renounce romance—and return with him to marry the aging nobleman to whom her father had pledged her.

Clearly she should say yes to Henry.
Clearly she should say no to Nicholas Bannion.
Except that when she looked closely at the man she so firmly believed she loved, and then into the eyes of the man she was sure she hated, nothing was clear at all. . . .

The
Runaway Bride

Other Regency Romances from SIGNET

The Runaway Bride

by
Sheila Walsh

A SIGNET BOOK
NEW AMERICAN LIBRARY
TIMES MIRROR

SIGNET, SIGNET CLASSIC, MENTOR, PLUME, MERIDIAN and NAL BOOKS
are published by The New American Library, Inc.,
1633 Broadway, New York, New York 10019

First Printing, October, 1983

1 2 3 4 5 6 7 8 9

PRINTED IN THE UNITED STATES OF AMERICA

Chapter 1

In the near-intolerable heat of an August afternoon two horses galloped across the scorched unyielding turf of the Sussex downs. The slighter of the two riders, finding a straggling clump of gorse in her path, put her sturdy mare at it and, with the skirt of her brown habit billowing, cleared it with an exuberant "Huzza!"

Her laughter floated joyously on the still air and Henry, Viscount Linton, following close on her heels, dabbed at the perspiration beading his brow, very much aware that with the ends of his crisply waving hair already clinging in limp, straw-colored wisps to his face, he was in imminent danger of losing the fashionable image of which he was so justifiably proud.

"Enough!" he cried at last in desperation. "Consuelo, you are the most complete hand! I can't think how you manage to raise so much energy in this abominably enervating heat."

In response, Consuelo Vasquez wrinkled her nose at him. It was a delightful nose, short and straight, flaring slightly above a willfully curving mouth.

"But then, mi Enrique, it is clear to me that you have never experienced Bilbao in the height of summer, for if you had, you would not find this present weather so intemperate."

"Maybe," admitted the young man, unconvinced. "But it ain't something I'd care to hazard money on. Anyway, I decree that we stop and rest for a while. See, there is a dew pond set in the shelter of that coppice yonder."

Without waiting for an answer, he urged his mount toward the welcoming shade, where he dismounted and turned to lift his companion down. Her waist was so tiny that his hands all but encompassed it as he swung her to the ground. Eyes as black and bright as ripe sloes looked wickedly aslant at him from under winged brows.

"It is well, I think, that Señora Diaz is prostrate with one of her bad headaches. She would be scandalized to know that I am riding with you . . . alone!"

"It would seem that your duenna suffers from a permanent state of the megrims. I have scarcely laid eyes on her in the two months you have been with Lady Covington."

"Poor Señora Diaz. She does not care for England. The customs are strange to her, and the food makes her ill." Consuelo flopped down without regard for her beautiful velvet skirt and leaned back on her hands, watching him. "Only two months! It does not seem possible. I can scarcely remember a time when I did not know you."

Henry, returning from watering and tethering the horses, found his blood stirring in his veins. He wondered if she knew how much allure was conveyed in that graceful unstudied pose. He had set out quite cynically to engage her affections and had succeeded with an ease that would have flattered his ego more had he not been aware that, unworldly as she was, she was ripe to be awakened.

What he had not expected was that he would enjoy the experience so much. It hardly seemed possible that this was the same girl who had arrived in London in June with her duenna—shy, repressed and at first disbelieving of the freedom permitted to English girls of her age. It had been amusing to draw her out, to play the romantic and watch the dawning of youthful adoration, to encourage her to throw off the inhibitions that prompted her to see all pleasure as a black sin. Soon she had blossomed beyond belief— sometimes a wayward innocent, sometimes incredibly mature for her years—a beautiful, tantalizing creature . . . and possessed of immensely rich father withal!

He crouched down and tipped the delicately pointed face up to him. "And I," he said, "can scarcely bear to contemplate a future without you."

Consuelo put up a hand swiftly to cover his. "It will not happen, *querido*," she told him confidently.

Moving her skirt aside, she patted the ground beside her and was amused when he spread a large silk handkerchief on the space before committing his spotless buff breeches to the turf. She teased him often about his concern with his dress, but oh, how she admired his handsomeness and his elegance!

"Have I not said?" she continued when he was comfortably settled beside her. "I mean to remain here in England so that we may be married."

"You have said it, my lovely Consuelo"—his lordship sighed—"but you are not free to choose, and if you were, what have I to offer you except my name? If you were not so absurdly young . . ."

"I am seventeen—almost eighteen years! In Spain that is not so young. . . ."

But she fell silent nonetheless, remembering that she should by now be back home in Bilbao, to be married on her birthday to the hateful Don Miguel Alphonso de Aranches, who was very old—almost as old as her father—and who wore corsets that creaked when he bowed. She had not seen Don Miguel since their betrothal when she was fifteen, and had resolutely put from her all thought of him and the faintly clammy touch of his fingers as he raised her chin to rake her with his snakelike eyes.

Until now. In these last weeks she had been forced to compare the fate intended for her with the almost unimaginable bliss of spending the rest of her life with Enrique. There was only one choice open to her.

Lord Linton observed the sudden pensive frown. "I am right, am I not, dearest? And there's the rub, for every time I see a carriage approaching the house, I fear that it will be your father come to carry you back to Spain."

Consuelo's profile took on an imperious tilt. "It will not be so, I promise you. My father will by now have received my letter, and Lord Covington has also written on our behalf. He thinks very well of Lord Covington, who was some kind of diplomat in Spain many years ago. They became friends, which is why my father permitted me to make this visit when my lord so kindly suggested it.

"So you see"—she laid a slim gloved hand on his arm—"by now it must be quite clear to him that my whole life is here with you. He cannot then force me into this marriage which is so utterly *repugnant* to me!" Consuelo's English had improved vastly during her stay and she delighted in the use of long words.

"I hope you are right."

"Of course I am right," she declared, confident once more. "You will see. We are indeed fortunate to have Lord and Lady Covington for our allies, are we not? Only consider, *querido*—if you had not been Lady Covington's very good friend, we might never have known one another!"

So diverted was she by this happy thought that she did not observe the telltale color that crept into his face. Abruptly he sprang to his feet.

"Come." He held out his hands. "We had better be on our way." His tawny eyes did not quite meet hers. "Don't want to take unwarranted advantage of our hosts."

They were within sight of Covington Manor when Consuelo lifted a hand to note the progress along the curving driveway of a gig drawn by a sedate brown horse. "See—my lady Covington has a visitor."

She turned her mount in the direction of the approaching gig, impelled by curiosity and a little by fear. For all her much-vaunted confidence she did not wish for a confrontation with her father. He was not slow to anger, and when roused he could be truly formidable.

Henry laid a restraining hand on her bridle, and as she turned to look at him, "Do you suppose . . .?" he began to say.

"No," she assured him. "I am quite certain that my father would never travel in so insignificant a carriage."

They both watched in silence as the gig drew to a halt before the imposing west front of the manor house with its four fine Corinthian columns. The figure that descended and ran up the steps was clearly that of a younger man than Consuelo's father.

"There! Did I not say?" Consuelo was triumphant in her relief. They set the horses in motion once more, the path leading them along between high yew hedges that masked the house from their view.

When it came once more into sight, the gig had gone. She sighed. "Quite clearly it was a person of no account."

Lady Covington was alone in the yellow drawing room when her butler, Hepworth, announced to her that there was a gentleman below seeking audience with his lordship. First instincts favored sending the visitor packing. Her husband could never be found when he was wanted, and she had no desire to entertain one of his dull cronies.

Verena Covington was filled with ennui. She was in that wearisome lull between the departure of one group of guests and the arrival of the next. Like the selfish, beautiful woman she was, she very quickly became bored without an audience to shower her with compliments, regale her with the latest scandals and generally relieve the tedium of the days between one London Season and the next—and in this capacity, Consuelo Vasquez and Henry Linton were less than useless, having become quite tiresomely engrossed in one another. But for the debilitating heat, she might have contemplated driving into Brighton.

She sighed and asked with an air of indifference, "What kind of a gentleman, Hepworth? Do we know him?"

"I think not, my lady." The butler looked vaguely disdainful. "A seafaring gentleman, I would hazard."

A gleam of interest flickered momentarily in her sleepy green eyes. "Really? A contemporary of his lordship's, would you say? An acquaintance from the late war, perhaps, though I am not aware that my husband had any particular friends in the navy."

Hepworth cleared his throat. "Begging your pardon, my lady, but I don't think . . . that is to say, I would not presume to class Captain Bannion as a contemporary of his lordship's . . . not in any way, if you follow me. The captain is a younger gentleman—very purposeful. Most insistent, in fact."

Lady Covington's silken lashes veiled her expression as she put up a limp hand to cover a yawn. She stretched herself languidly. "Well, I suppose I had better see him. You may show him up, Hepworth—and send someone to find Lord Covington. They might try the gamekeeper's cottage. I believe he spoke of calling there."

As the door closed behind the butler she rose and crossed the room to stand before one of the three pier glasses which ornamented the spaces between the windows. The reflection also showed the white and gold furnishings—a perfect setting, it could not be denied, for a creature once dubbed by the Prince Regent "an Aphrodite among women." That was some years ago, it was true, but her looks were, if anything, better than ever now.

When Captain Bannion was admitted, she was standing by the window just where the sun filtered through the muslin curtains to make an aura of light about her red-gold hair.

As they exchanged greetings, she saw at once why Hepworth had been faintly disparaging. The captain was a very physical man, not destined to shine in a lady's drawing room; not more than thirty, she decided, and a little above medium height, he had the deeply bronzed look of a man more used to spending his time in the open air. Yet for all that, his coat was well cut—by Scott, perhaps, for it certainly did not bear Weston's stamp—though it was clear that he favored comfort rather than elegance since it had been made so that he could shrug himself into it without assistance. And his buckskins displayed an excellent leg.

Also, he did have the most devastatingly blue, blue eyes, Verena decided as she gestured gracefully for him to be seated—thickly lashed eyes with interesting creases at the corners and an intolerance in their depths that was echoed in the thrust of his jaw as he made his bow. Her interest was aroused.

"Is your business with my husband of a confidential nature, Captain Bannion?" she inquired huskily as he took the chair opposite her.

"No, ma'am. I daresay it concerns you quite as much as his lordship. More so, perhaps." His voice was firm, crisp—the voice of a man accustomed to giving orders and being obeyed without question. "I am here on behalf of Señor Vasquez. He is much vexed by his daughter's continuing absence from home." His keen eyes challenged her. "I understand she was to have returned home several weeks since."

"That is true." She met his glance with limpid innocence. "But surely Consuelo wrote to her father to explain. My husband also. Has the good señor not received these letters?"

"He has." The captain's tone was curt. "It is as a direct result of receiving them that I am here now to escort Señorita Vasquez home without further delay. I must ask you, ma'am, to summon her—and her duenna—so that arrangements may be put in hand."

Lady Covington raised her finely plucked brows in amused surprise. "Just like that, Captain?"

"My time is precious, ma'am. I have commitments . . ."

"Maybe so. But, my dear sir, you cannot uproot a young girl at a moment's notice, especially one of Consuelo's temperament, without inviting severe repercussions!" She shrugged. "I will not pretend that I have not expected something of this nature, though I had supposed Señor Vasquez would wish to deal with the matter personally."

"Had it been possible, he would have done so. Regrettably, the señor's health at the present time precludes any undue exertion."

"I see. And so he sends you." She spoke as though the thought amused her.

It did not, however, amuse him. "No one sends me anywhere, Lady Covington. I agreed to lend Señor Vasquez my support in this affair because we have been acquainted for many years, because he was ill and distressed and because the speedy return of his daughter is of paramount importance to him. It touches upon his honor."

"Well then." She shrugged again. "You will have some form of authorization, I presume?"

"I have." He didn't offer to produce it and she was not really interested. She had no wish to involve herself with tiresome details. She rose unhurriedly.

Her silk skirts swished softly as she moved about the room, and Captain Bannion, coming to his feet also, watched her with a kind of cynical amusement, aware that she was aware that he watched.

"Señor Vasquez will have told you, I suppose, that the child fancies herself in love?"

"At seventeen?" His mouth curled derisively. "Romantic twaddle, ma'am. In twelve months' time, I doubt she will even recall the young man's name."

"Oh, fie, sir!" Verena whisked across the room, a subtle fragrance teasing his nostrils as she swayed perilously close to him, her beautiful green eyes lifted provocatively to his. "Have you no heart? Would you wrest so lovely and spirited a creature from the arms of her Adonis? For young Henry Linton *is* quite distractingly handsome, as well as being perfectly eligible. His father is the Earl of Gratton. Consuelo could do a lot worse!"

He was not in the least disconcerted by her nearness; rather, he seemed to be enjoying the experience. "It would make no difference. The girl's future is already decided."

"The fat, elderly Spaniard?" She wrinkled her nose distastefully. "I have heard of him." She sighed deeply, displaying a tantalizing glimpse of milk-white breasts. "Such a pity! But then, I know what it is to be married to an older man!"

Nick Bannion was no stranger to women and he knew well enough that he was being offered a none-too-subtle invitation. For a moment he even entertained the possibility of taking it up—the lady was obviously much pampered—and bored! Reluctantly he remembered his mission.

She sensed his withdrawal and flounced away, her lip caught vexatiously between even, white teeth. It was perhaps fortunate, however, for almost immediately the door opened to admit a large genial man busily engaged in mopping his face with a spotted handkerchief.

"Well now, m'dear. Hepworth tells me we've a visitor." Lord Covington's amiable glance shifted to Captain Bannion as his wife performed the introductions. "Servant, Captain. Hepworth is on his way with some refreshment. You'll take a glass of Madeira, eh?"

"With pleasure, my lord."

"Stout fellow!" His lordship ran the handkerchief around the back of his neck and stufffed it untidily into the pocket of his once-elegant frock coat. "This heat—quite insupportable, what? Now then, my dear sir, sit down. Make yourself comfortable and tell me how I may serve you."

Nick Bannion explained his mission yet again, as succinctly as possible, while being made very much aware of Lady Covington's eyes resting on him. He wondered briefly what had made her marry a man who must surely exasperate her with every breath he drew.

"D'ye mean you're to take our little Consuelo away?" Lord Covington wheezed, fumbling for his snuff box. "Oh, come now, sir!"

At this point Hepworth entered with a tray, and there was some little delay as the drinks were poured and served. As he left, Hepworth was instructed by her ladyship to ask the Señorita Vasquez to step up to the drawing room the moment she returned from her ride.

"She'll not take it kindly, m'dear." Lord Covington cast a meaningful glance at his wife.

"Oh, Captain Bannion knows all about Henry, do you not, sir?"

Nick inclined his head, refusing the snuff offered to him.

"Bannion?" mused his lordship. "You wouldn't be *the* Bannion . . . the one involved with young Cochrane in that spot of bother in the Basque roads? Eighteen-oh-nine, wasn't it?"

"Best chance we ever had to blast the French fleet out of existence!" Nick Bannion's eyes sparkled with anger, remembering.

"By George! It *was* you!"

Lady Covington, her interest aroused, listened with veiled eyes as her husband waxed enthusiastic.

"It was the damndest thing I ever heard tell of, m'dear! Night as black as the devil, storm raging, and the French holed up safely under the protection of the shore batteries . . . or so they thought, what?" He chuckled and continued, oblivious of the younger man's discouraging expression. "But they'd reckoned without Lord Cochrane, and Bannion here. . . . With a few chosen men they ran the best part of twenty fireships and explosion vessels inshore right under the noses of the enemy . . . wreaked havoc . . . set most of the French ships hopelessly adrift . . ."

"We didn't succeed as well as we'd hoped," said Nick, drawn reluctantly to intervene. "The weather was against us. But we could still have finished them off come daylight if that pious, psalm-singing purist, Gambier, hadn't sat on the horizon with the fleet, ignoring Cochrane's signals that the French were at our mercy!" Nick's lips twisted. "Lord Gambier didn't approve our brief, you see—not quite the thing, attacking your enemy at night! Also he deeply resented Lord Cochrane's being sent to supersede him! By the time we stung him into action by going it alone, it was almost too late. And soon after, the admiral called off the action. Cochrane was so angry, he demanded a court-martial!"

He had said much more than he'd meant to, and was very much aware of Lady Covington's eyes resting on him with an amused, calculating expression. It threw him on to the defensive, the more so as Lord Covington continued jovially, "That's right! And Gambier was cleared and everyone spoke of the action as a great victory . . . enemy ships destroyed and all that! Well, I never! And later, as I recall, you were put ashore somewhere around that area and spent some time in the mountains with a party of brigands." He blew his nose. "Well, now . . . we must talk more about this after dinner, what? You'll be staying for dinner, of course?" He looked to his wife.

She said smoothly, "Naturally, we should be delighted to have you stay, Captain." Her voice lifted with faint irony. "I had no idea we were entertaining one of England's heroes!"

"Nothing of the kind, ma'am," said the captain stiffly. "As to dinner, I regret—"

There came an interruption in the form of a light rap on the door. It was flung open to admit a tiny glowing figure in rich brown velvet, a froth of lace at her throat, her dark eyes brilliant.

"Dear Lady Covington, Hepworth has said that you wish to see me. We have had a splendid ride . . ." Consuelo's voice trailed away as she saw that her ladyship was not alone. "Oh, forgive me, I did not know . . ." Again the words dried up as a man rose from the chair opposite and turned—broadshouldered, black-browed—to face her, a man looking curiously out of place in the lovely white-and-gold drawing room. And surely something about him was familiar to her?

Lady Covington extended a graceful hand. "Come, child, and be introduced." She smiled encouragingly. "But then, perhaps no introduction will be necessary. Captain Bannion, my dear, is a friend of your father."

Consuelo stared blankly as he bowed.

"Good afternoon, Señorita Vasquez." His voice was dry. "I am sorry to break in upon your pleasures with such distressing abruptness, but I have come to take you home to your father."

Chapter 2

There was a curious little silence during which Nick waited with frowning formality, betraying nothing of his surprise. Consuelo's father had said that she was beautiful, but he, having only the vaguest memory of her as a child, had thought it to be no more than the natural partiality of a parent for his only daughter.

But Consuelo *was* beautiful. And watching the proud head thrown back, he had little doubt that the rest of the parental prophecy would prove equally accurate, for, "Alas, Señor Bannion," her father had said resignedly, sighing, "she can also be distressingly willful!" And there was surely stubbornness in the thrust of that full lower lip. He was already regretting his quixotic offer of help.

Consuelo meanwhile stood unmoving, a great fear clutching at her stomach. She looked to Lady Covington—exquisitely fair, exquisitely lovely, her green eyes a little pitying as she lifted her shoulders in an elegant little shrug. She looked to Lord Covington, standing ill at ease before the fireplace, and in his face read embarrassment and a certain distress. As for Captain Bannion, he simply watched her impassively. No pity there, no help, no hope. Her fear grew—and with it came a great anger.

"This I do not believe!" she cried. "My father would not send such a one as you to do this thing!"

The captain's face wore its most shuttered look. "Believe what you will, señorita, it is the truth, and you had better accept it. I am a busy man and have little time to pander to tantrums." He paused and seemed to be choosing his words with care. "In fact, your father is ill and your recent irresponsible behavior has done little to improve his health. Does it concern you at all, I wonder, to learn that by your actions you are causing him a considerable amount of unnecessary suffering?"

A little color came up under the pale olive skin and faded almost as it came. She would not be taken to task by this man who was little more than a common sailor. How dare he look at her as though she were *malvada*—a wicked, recalcitrant child! She drew herself up very straight and looked down her nose at him with as much hauteur as she could command.

"I am sorry that my father is unwell, Captain. He knows, I hope, that I would never willingly cause him one moment of grief."

But he was growing impatient of so much argument. "I have no wish to listen to your protestations of regret, señorita," he said curtly. "You may save them until you are able to deliver them in person."

"Ah, no!"

"For the present I would like to speak with your duenna," he continued inexorably, looking her over with critical eyes and remembering the two figures he had seen riding across the fields with such intimacy as he had driven up. "It would seem that the señora has been lax in her duties."

"Señora Diaz is indisposed, Captain Bannion," Lady Covington interposed smoothly. There was a faint

mocking light in her eyes, as though she found the
whole episode a little absurd. "I fear she has been
unwell almost from the day she arrived. I am sorry if
you feel we have failed in our care of Consuelo, for
she has become as a daughter to us, has she not, my
lord?"

"By Jupiter, yes!" Lord Covington stumbled over
the words, the glance he directed at Consuelo plainly
showing his adoration. "Delightful little creature! Not
a scrap of trouble! I am sure, my love, that the good
captain ain't in any way casting doubt upon our care
of Consuelo."

His wife threw him a look of thinly veiled contempt,
which did not escape Nick. A charming pair, he
decided, growing impatient once more. His voice
was clipped.

"I accuse no one of anything, my lord. All I ask is
that Señora Diaz be exhorted to bestir herself in
order that she may make ready to accompany her
charge. I have a crew kicking its heels at Plymouth
and a cargo awaiting delivery. My time is valuable. I
wish to leave for Spain as soon as possible!"

"Leave?" cried Consuelo. "No! I will not leave this
place without my Enrique!" She ran to Lord Covington, flinging out her hands to him imploringly. "Dear
lord, tell him that it is not possible!"

"There, there, child!" Lord Covington gathered
her hands into his, patting them awkwardly and looking more than anything like a distressed sheepdog.
"Come now, Captain," he blustered. "You are being
overhard on this dear creature! You can see how it is
with her—so deep in love with young Linton and he
with her—quite affecting to behold, y'know!"

"I don't know," said Nick dryly. "Fortunately I am
not so easily swayed."

"*Insensato!*" Consuelo turned scornful, tear-drenched

eyes upon him. "What would you know of such a love?"

"Oh, for pity's sake, spare me any more of this Cheltenham tragedy!" Nick turned to Lady Covington, the only other person to appear unmoved by so much passion; indeed, he thought, she seemed amused by all the fuss. "Madam, perhaps you can instill a little sense into this child?"

"I am not a child!"

Her ladyship's brows arched delicately. "Perhaps, sir, you might show a little more tolerance." As he flushed angrily she turned to Consuelo. "My dear, Captain Bannion is acting for your father. If he insists that you return home, there is little that any of us can do."

"No doubt he is being well paid for his services!" came the scathing retort. "Is that not so, Captain?"

The creases about his eyes came together, narrowing them to angry slits, but he would not be drawn. Consuelo gathered the remnants of her pride.

"Well, it matters little, for I will not go with you." She turned on her trimly booted heel and marched to the door.

"Señorita!" His voice—the voice his crew knew so well—stopped her before she ever reached it. "I have a letter here for you from your father. I advise you to read it and digest its contents well."

Consuelo came back, reluctantly, stiff-backed, and with a commendable degree of composure held out her hand for the letter, looked at it and then at him. "You know it's contents?"

"I do. Briefly, it requires that from this moment you obey me in all things as you would your father until you are once more beneath his roof."

She stared at him, tore open the letter and devoured its contents at a glance. A tight band constricted her chest, her breath seemed to be forced unevenly from an aching throat. "No! *Absolutemente*, no! I will never submit to you!"

They stood very close, glittering blue eyes locked with flagrantly defiant black ones. Then:

"Oh, but you will," he said with a soft vehemence that was more disturbing than mere anger, "because I am not your father, or Lord Covington, or even that young puppy with whom you fancy yourself in love, to be twisted round your little finger. Because however much you rail at me, or sulk or seek to cajole me, you will not move me one jot!"

A moment more their glances held—and it was Consuelo who broke first. Without another word, she drew a sobbing breath and fled from the room, picking up her skirts as she passed a startled footman, and rushed headlong for the stairs.

In the drawing room, the vacuum left by her abrupt departure was filled by Lord Covington's blustering protestations until he was silenced by a look from his wife.

She said with mild exasperation: "Well, sir, that was an ill-managed business. And I took you for a man of sense! You may be a most excellent leader of men, but you have a remarkably clumsy hand when it comes to dealing with a mere slip of a girl!"

Anger flared and then died in his eyes, to be replaced by a brief ironical smile. "I did make a sad botch of it, didn't I? But, dammit, I had no idea she was such a little hellcat!"

Lady Covington's smile was sympathetic. "Well, but what did you expect? That she would submit meekly to your edict? Consuelo is a young woman of spirit, but not a hellcat, I promise you. Still, it is not too late to make amends."

His look was guarded. "I will not go back on what I said."

"Of course not. One could not expect you to do so," she agreed soothingly. "But if you were to be a little conciliating . . . if you could, perhaps, give the child a day or two in which to grow used to the idea . . ." As he opened his mouth to protest, her husky laugh stopped him. "Oh, come, Captain, you must appreciate what a shock this has been for Consuelo. We had so many things planned!"

"Maybe, but . . ."

"I know what you are going to say—your ship and your horrid old commitments!" With a look she silenced her husband again as he was about to intervene. "But surely," she continued persuasively, "your cargo will wait a day or two, and I am quite certain that your crew will not cavil at the prospect of a few days more ashore?"

"I am sure they will not!" he agreed dryly, and there was a gleam in his eyes. "What I was about to say, ma'am, is that I very much doubt whether the kind of delay you speak of will alter the señorita's mind for the better."

"Leave Consuelo to me." She sensed that he was wavering and gave him her most charming smile. "How would it be if you were to stay, say until the weekend? I have some guests arriving tomorrow, and we are having a ball on Friday evening. Consuelo has been so looking forward to it. And you must stay here, naturally. . . ."

"Ah, as to that, ma'am, I have my room booked at the Ship in Brighton. It was their gig I hired to come up here today."

"Oh, all that can easily be taken care of, Captain! So, what do you say?"

He knew well that he was being cozened, yet he

found himself saying with a wry grin, "You make it very hard for me to refuse without appearing boorish, ma'am. Very well, I agree—but only until Saturday. I can stretch matters no further." He turned to Lord Covington. "Your wife has a most persuasive tongue, sir."

His lordship brushed away the inevitable trickle of snuff from his coat and gave him a sanguine look from under bushy brows. "Oh, aye," he said. "I never knew her not to get anything once she's set her mind to't."

There was a touch of asperity in Lady Covington's voice, though she laughed. "Fie, my lord, you make me sound like a . . . a scheming jade! Take no notice of him, Captain. All will work out splendidly. You will have time to become better acquainted with Consuelo. I give you my word, she is a delightful girl!"

The delightful girl was, at that moment, in her own bedchamber, flung down upon her bed in a storm of weeping. It was a most attractive room, done over in yellow and white, and now, with the sun pouring in, looking at its best. But Consuelo was for once blind to its charms as she pummeled the pretty sprigged counterpane with clenched fists in a passion of mingled grief and temper.

Her maidservant, Maria, looked on with sympathetic concern. As was usually the case, word had traveled quickly among the servants that a gentleman had arrived to take her mistress back to Spain. But the gentleman was not, as Maria had been expecting, Señor Vasquez.

Having been with the Señorita Consuelo from her earliest days, she had been prepared for tantrums, but never before had she witnessed such an abandonment to weeping. Maria sighed. Of course, one knew well enough the cause! The Lord Linton was a young gentleman of such handsomeness—and of so romantic a disposition! Had not her mistress a whole sheaf of poems tucked beneath her pillow at this very moment—paeans of praise to her eyes, to the passing grace of her dainty feet, even to the ground they walked upon! Who would not weep to exchange such flights of passion for the cold proud arrogance of Don Miguel, fine match though he undoubtedly was.

She regarded her own plain scrubbed countenance in the looking glass and sighed lustily. Would that someone might pen such love poems to her! And yet—words were small comfort on a cold night. She had curves enough, and in the darkness a man might forget a plain face.

Maria leaned over the bed and stroked the sable hair, shaken loose from its pins. "Do not weep so, señorita," she pleaded. "You will make yourself ill!"

"I do not care! I wish only to die! Yes"—Consuelo lifted her head to sob tragically at the shocked maid—"that is it . . . I will kill myself, and then they will all repent of their cruelty, but it will be in vain!" Her glance fell upon the exquisite ballgown of cream silk trimmed with Valenciennes lace which was hanging outside the closet ready for Lady Covington's ball. "Ah, but then no one will see my pretty dress! Ah, Maria—what am I to do?" Suddenly she scrambled upright and smote her forehead. "*Estupida!* Of course. I must see Enrique. Maria, you will take a note to him without delay."

There came a sharp little rap on the door and Lady Covington swept in, trailing her pale silk skirts. She signaled for the maid to leave.

"Well, child, you *have* set the place in a pucker!" She sank gracefully on to the bed beside Consuelo, reflecting with some irritation how incredibly lovely the little Spanish girl contrived to look after a bout of weeping which would have left most women with swollen eyes and a blotched skin. In Consuelo, the dark brooding eyes merely grew larger and more luminous; a flush added a faint dusting of color to the pale olive skin, but this merely emphasized in a most provoking manner her beautiful high cheekbones.

Verena Covington decided that she really would not be sorry to see Consuelo go. Who could have guessed that the quiet, grave-eyed girl who had arrived from Spain but two months since with her duenna would so soon blossom into a vivacious young woman who was already attracting a deal more attention than could rightly be tolerated.

That was why she had thrown Henry Linton into Consuelo's path. His passionate attachment to Verena herself had become a trifle tedious; besides which, though her husband was remarkably obtuse, it might well prove awkward were he to suspect that he was being cuckolded by a much younger man—and under his own roof at that.

It had been simple enough to impress Henry with the size of Señor Vasquez's fortune—and Consuelo his only daughter. Henry had for some time been living beyond his means; and with little immediate prospect of recouping his resources, it had not been too difficult to persuade him that an advantageous marriage was the answer to his problem, and that, notwithstanding the presence of a Spanish fiancé, Consuelo could be his for the asking. Still, it had been somewhat galling to note the alacrity with which he had transferred his attentions to Consuelo. But it reassured her to command his homage from time to time and see how easily he could still be enslaved.

A touch on her arm recalled her to the matter in hand.

"Dear Lady Covington, tell me what I am to do," pleaded Consuelo. "I cannot go with that man when my whole happiness is here."

Verena, knowing exactly what she intended her to do, paved the way with skill. "Do you think that if Henry went to see your father, perhaps . . .? He is not a nobody, after all. He may be a trifle short of funds at the present, but one day, you know, he will be the Earl of Gratton."

Consuelo shook her head vigorously, and the cloud of shining sable hair lifted and settled again about her face. She pushed it back impatiently. "It would make no difference, señora. I am promised to Don Miguel, who is humorless and arrogant and incredibly old!" The words rang like a knell. "In my country such a promise is binding unto death—and if I am forced to marry Don Miguel instead of Enrique I think that I *shall* die!"

Lady Covington had little patience with histrionics, but she did not allow this to show. "Then we must ensure that you do not have to marry him."

"I do not understand . . ."

Her ladyship rose and crossed to the mirror, where she turned this way and that, surveying herself critically, not unpleased with what she saw. "You are but an infant in your dealings with men, my dear. Captain Bannion, for example . . ."

"I hate him!" Consuelo spat the words.

"You have made that abundantly clear," said Lady Covington dryly. "But you will never get the better of a man like the captain with such tactics. You should be thanking me, you know. I have been working very hard on your behalf."

Consuelo slid from the bed and went hopefully to

her side. Verena Covington did not like the joint reflection half so well and turned abruptly away. "You have made him change his mind?" the girl asked.

This was greeted with a light trill of laughter. "My dear, I am not quite a miracle worker!" And as Consuelo's expression fell: "But I have been rather clever, I think. I have persuaded the good captain that he has been less than fair to you and that he should postpone his departure until the morning following my ball."

"I do not see how that can do any good," said Consuelo.

"Oh, come now—only think! A lot can happen in two days. I see no reason why you and Henry, if you give your minds to it, should not outwit Captain Bannion."

Consuelo's dark eyes grew round and then began to sparkle. "You mean . . . elope?" She said the word half fearfully. "Can we do such a thing?"

"It is your only chance," said Lady Covington bluntly. "But it must be planned with care. You may leave that to me. I shall speak to Henry . . ."

"May I see him, please?"

"Later, child. I will arrange it. But from now until Friday, you must do exactly as I tell you. It is settled that Captain Bannion will stay here for the remainder of his visit—I have persuaded him that it will give him the chance to know you better. What I wish of you is that you behave as though you are growing resigned to your lot. Can you do that?"

"But, yes!" Consuelo danced around the room in an ecstasy of joy as the idea took shape in her mind, coming at last to kneel at Lady Covington's side, lifting her hand dramatically to kiss her dress. "If you can do this thing for us, dear Lady Covington, we shall bless you forever!" She rose, all hauteur. "And I shall play my part when I meet the wicked captain with gr-reat conviction, you will see! I shall be heartbroken, but terribly brave!"

"Yes, well don't overdo it, my dear. I think perhaps for this evening it might be more prudent, and more in keeping with your state of mind, if you do not come downstairs for dinner."

Verena Covington was herself stirred to a strange excitement at the thought of outwitting the captain; intrigue had ever been the breath of life to her. She liked to court danger and she sensed that Captain Bannion would be a dangerous man to cross, but an exciting one to know, for all that. And she could not but be aware that he found her attractive. . . .

"Do you know anything of Captain Bannion's background?" she asked casually, pleating her skirt with fingers that shook very slightly. "It might be as well to know where we stand with him."

The scowl returned to Consuelo's face. "I know very little, for although he came sometimes to the house, I seldom encountered him. I believe Maria once told me that his mother was from a family of great nobility in Valencia. There was much talk among the servants that a person with such connections should be a mere sea captain. . . ." A gleam came into her eyes. "Perhaps they disowned him because he was not enough respectable!"

Verena moved impatiently. "And yet your father thinks well enough of him to entrust him with the safe return of his daughter?"

"Captain Bannion carries all my father's merchandise," said Consuelo hotly. "No doubt he regards me in a similar light!"

"That is no way to speak of your father." Lady Covington's reproof was chilling.

"No. I am sorry, but it is not easy for me to think well of him when he sends such a one for me . . . a nobody that he knows only from the war."

"The captain is not exactly a nobody. My husband tells me that his father is Sir Patrick Bannion, a most charming rake . . . though with nary a penny to bless himself with. I had no idea *he* had a son!"

"Well, I cannot see that it helps at all to know these things," Consuelo reasoned. "If we are to outwit him, we will have to be very clever, for I expect that he can be quite ruthless. He lived and fought with the *guerrilleros* in the mountains during the war you know." Consuelo gave a pugnacious little nod. "*That* would suit him very well, I think!"

"Oh yes, it would," murmured Lady Covington.

Chapter 3

It was not easy for Consuelo to remain quietly in her room. Now that she had hope, she wanted to be doing something useful toward hastening the hour when she and her beloved Enrique could run away. But Lady Covington had been most severe with her about not doing anything to spoil her plans, so she must be patient. She changed her riding dress for a gown of jonquil-colored muslin with a high waist and tiny puff sleeves, and for some time lay on the bed reading the pretty verses Henry had composed for her. But when her duenna demanded to see her, most unexpectedly, she was obliged to push the pages quickly under the covers.

Señora Diaz had herself been summoned from her couch when Captain Bannion curtly insisted upon seeing her. She had presented herself to him in a small insignificant saloon at the rear of the house (an indignity that did not escape her) dressed in her habitual black, and draped in a quantity of shawls, notwithstanding the heat of the day.

She had listened, sour-faced but impassive, to his opinions of her laxness in her duties to her charge and, at the end of an uncomfortable ten minutes, was left in little doubt that he considered her guilty of

negligence. He had concluded by exhorting her coolly
to bestir herself.

"You have time yet to redeem yourself, señora,
for I am looking to you to ensure that Señorita Vasquez
is ready and at least outwardly compliant about un-
dertaking the journey home on Saturday."

Not unnaturally, this reprimand from a stranger,
an ill-mannered man whom she considered in every
way her inferior, did not sit well with Señora Diaz,
who proceeded to vent her spleen in the only way
open to her.

For some time she harangued Consuelo in a plaintive monotone for her base ingratitude, her want of
decorum, the ruthless way in which she had made
use of her duenna's state of collapse in order to
pursue her own selfish pleasures.

"Did I not warn how it would be?" Two button-
black eyes burned self-righteously in the recesses
of her pallid, overplump face. "And now what
comes to me? I must return to face your father, for
you have called down his wrath, not only upon your
own head, but upon mine also! And I know not what
is to become of me if I am turned off. . . ."

Consuelo might have been incensed had she not
been so preoccupied by the important problems of
planning an elopement; besides, she had heard it all
before—many times. So she contented herself with a
murmured "si señora" whenever a pause seemed to
indicate that some kind of answer was required of
her.

When, however, the duenna's fingers fastened cruelly on her arm in order to emphasize a point, the
young girl drew herself up very straight and demanded coldly that she unhand her.

It was too much; like a pricked bubble, Señora
Diaz stopped in midsentence on an angry sob and,

exhausted by so much unaccustomed effort, departed in order to recruit her strength for the ordeals ahead by means of the dish of sugared plums that Lady Covington had so kindly sent to her room.

Consuelo's plotting was once more interrupted when Maria came to say that Lady Covington desired to have words with her in her boudoir, but this interruption she did not mind, for there, in her ladyship's boudoir, her Enrique awaited her. She flew into his arms with a joyful cry, and he gathered her to him with all the ardor for which her romantic soul yearned.

"Ah, my dearest love, how I wish I had been there to support you," he whispered into her ear. "But, have no fear, the arrogant captain shall not be permitted to carry you off in such a cavalier fashion!"

Consuelo's eyes widened; a tiny frisson of fear ran down her back. "You would make him fight you? Oh, but you must not!" In the pages of a novel, a duel was very acceptable, but in reality . . She struggled from his arms and turned to Lady Covington, who was reclining upon her chaise-longue in a pale pink negligee, watching them with a slight frown puckering her brow. "My lady, he must not fight Captain Bannion, must he?"

"Certainly not." Lady Covington's voice was cool. "Henry knows well enough that I will have no brawling in my house."

"Well, how do you expect me to behave when I meet him?" demanded Henry, with the air of one determined to give his all. "Should I be civil when I know he means to carry Consuelo away very much against her will? A poor sort of lover I should be if I did not challenge him!"

It was pure bravura. Lady Covington, knowing that a duel was the very last thing Henry would wish for, glanced at Consuelo's glowing face and contented

herself with an exasperated: "You will do as I tell
you, Henry, or you are like to ruin everything. Now
let us all sit down calmly, and I will tell you both
what I think you should do."

Henry shrugged resignedly, and Consuelo, supposing that her beloved was bruised in spirit, seized his
hand impulsively and pressed it against her cheek.

"I am very proud, *amigo,* that you wish to fight
this man for me, but I would so much rather that you
did not get yourself killed!"

Her words ruffled his feelings somewhat. "I am
generally reckoned to be a pretty fair shot," he declared pettishly.

"Yes, but Señor Bannion fought with the *guerrilleros*
and will very likely be a better one," she reasoned,
and added, as a thought struck her: "Besides which, it
is entirely possible that he might cheat"

"Consuelo!" Exasperation was threatening to get
the better of Lady Covington. "Please to come and
sit down." She swung her feet gracefully to the
floor and patted the place beside her on the chaise-
longue. Consuelo sat and Henry took the ridiculously
fragile-looking chair opposite them.

"That is better," Lady Covington pronounced. "Now
then, Consuelo. Between us, Henry and I have
evolved a plan, which, if everyone plays their parts
as I hope they will, should give you an excellent
chance of deceiving Captain Bannion for as long as it
takes you to make good your escape. But it involves
the exercise of patience." She looked severely at
them both.

"I still think we should go tonight," said Henry
with unexpected obstinacy. "Can't see the value in
kicking our heels here for another couple of days—
having to be polite to that man!"

"You are right, *querido.*" In her enthusiasm

Consuelo could not remain quiet. "I, also, have been giving the matter much consideration and I have thought of a splendid plan! It is really very simple. As soon as everyone is in bed tonight we can drive away in your curricle—and I will be your tiger. That boy of yours, Green—he shall lend me one of his suits. His livery will look very well on me, do you not think?"

She saw her beloved frown. "Or would you prefer that we ride?" She shrugged. "It is all one to me."

But this was going too far to suit Henry's notions of propriety. "Certainly not! I could not possibly permit . . ."

Consuelo looked at him sitting there on the pretty little gilt chair in his beautiful blue coat and yellow pantaloons, his cravat a marvelously discreet confection, a faint look of distaste marring the handsome features. Her eyes danced. "Oh, Enrique, I have shocked you! But indeed, you must not be! An elopement should also be an adventure. Am I not right, Lady Covington?"

She swung round and encountered a shaft of anger which astonished her. Her ladyship's patience was at an end. She had everything so beautifully worked out—had even managed to persuade Captain Bannion to stay at Covington Mannor. She had met every problem that he had put in the way—so much did she wish to exploit that gleam of desire she had glimpsed in his eyes. He was quite unlike any man she had ever known; the merest conjecture as to how it would be to be possessed by such a man set her senses in a turmoil.

Now these two silly children were like to wreck all her plans. She didn't much care whether their hopes were blighted eventually; in point of fact, she would be very much surprised if they were capable of outwitting a man like Bannion for long, but if they took it into their hands to run off prematurely, he would go after them and that would probably be the last she would see of him. Her schemes would count for nought.

"Can you think of no one but yourselves?" she demanded. "Do you realize how long I have spent in preparations for my ball on Friday evening? Over two hundred guests are invited. Hugh is hopeful of persuading Prinny to attend. And all will be wrecked if you are minded to be selfish." They both looked so astonished that she forced herself to be calm. Her beautiful green eyes reproached them gently. "Is it so much to ask that you wait a little longer?"

Consuelo was immediately contrite. 'Dear Lady Covington, you have been so good, so kind! We will do whatever you think best." She looked at Henry severely. "Will we not, *querido?*"

He eyed Verena sardonically, as though deeply suspicious of her motives, but he knew himself to be powerless against the two of them. He shrugged assent.

"That is better," Lady Covington said, mollified. "I promise you it is for the best. And, you know, I do believe Consuelo's idea of taking Green's place is an excellent one. It will make tracing you that much more difficult. But you will not leave until just before dawn on the Saturday morning. Everyone will by then be asleep. You, my dear Consuelo, will plead tiredness at midnight. Yes, my dear," she insisted as the girl looked set to argue, "for you will need go get a little sleep. Is your maid to be trusted?"

"Oh, Maria will do anything I ask of her," said Consuelo confidently. "She is devoted to me!"

"Good. That will be useful. But not a word to her beforehand." Lady Covington yawned delicately and stood up. "And now, my dears, you must go away so that I may finish dressing for dinner. The Fossbury's are expected, also Madame Garrishe."

"Oh," said Consuelo, aggrieved. "I shall be very sorry to miss Madame."

"Never mind, child, you will see her on Friday evening. Now, do run along."

By the time her dinner was sent up on a tray, Consuelo was ravenous. Maria was quite astonished to see how quickly everything set before her was eaten and enjoyed without a murmur. When it was made known that she was taking dinner in her room, Maria had expected that the food would be picked at, especially in view of all the upset and the heartbreak that had been so apparent earlier . . . though to be sure a change had come over her mistress after Lady Covington had spoken with her. But no amount of probing on the maid's part could elicit from Consuelo anything other than a mischievous grin.

"I shall take a walk in the garden," she informed Maria after prowling around the room restlessly for some time.

"But, señorita—it is almost dark!"

"So? What has that to say to anything? The air will still be warm—and much fresher than during the day."

"Do you wish that I accompany you?" asked the reluctant maid, who, believing that her mistress would be occupied elsewhere, had already planned an assignation with the second footman.

"Certainly not." Consuelo was very definite. "I wish to be quite by myself."

Maria's eyes opened a little wider. Could the señorita be plotting something? With the second footman still in mind, Maria decided that it was not her place to interfere.

The evening air enfolded Consuelo with all the softness of the fine lacy shawl she had draped about her shoulders. The varied scents of Lady Covington's herb garden were sweet in her nostrils as she wandered past them toward the east front of the house. The last of the sunset had now faded, and looking down to the lake she saw a row of poplar etched in black silhouette against sky paled to that shade of calm clear turquoise that precedes the velvety blackness of night. From the uncurtained windows of the drawing room, light poured out over the great curving semicircle of balustraded steps, spilling down on to the terrace below and trickling away over the lush green lawns to disappear into the indistinct grayness beyond.

Inside the drawing room the company would be laughing and talking, enjoying themselves—probably without a thought for her. Consuelo felt dejected and quite irrationally deprived. Would they miss her, any of these people, when she was no longer here? She thought not. It had been the strangest day, a day filled with every emotion from elation to abject misery; now, with all passion spent, she felt unaccountably flat.

Her thoughts turned irresistibly to home. It distressed her that she must go against her father's will. It was not that she did not love him, she argued, though love in her case had always been born of duty and tinged with a kind of awe. She remembered when, as a child, she had longed to fling herself into his arms, but there had always been that curious formality in his manner, an aloofness about the neat elegance of his figure, his ascetic features and small neat beard, which inhibited her from any show of affection. Would he have been different, she wondered, had her mother lived?

That he was proud of her—and of her budding beauty—was made evident when he presented her to anyone, but it was admiration of the kind that he reserved for any beautiful object. And yet, perhaps he did love her in his own way. Was it this thought which prompted the sudden guilt that assailed her . . . the possibility that she might have contributed by her behavior to this illness of which Captain Bannion had spoken—might even have been its cause?

The wetness of tears was on her cheeks as she walked well out across the lawns where the lights from the house could not pick out her pale, wraithlike figure drifting toward the deep umbrella shadow of a spreading Cypress tree.

She had almost reached it when a faint whiff of smoke tingled in her nostrils. Someone was leaning, arms folded, against the tree's ample trunk. She could clearly discern the glowing tip of a cigar, a curl of smoke and the white blur of a gentleman's shirt. Her step faltered, for something in that arrogant casual stance was familiar. First instincts urged flight, but she would not give him that satisfaction. She stopped just short of the tree and saw that he had discarded his coat and cravat and that his shirt was unbuttoned at the throat. Through the curling cigar smoke, he regarded her with narrowed eyes.

Nick Bannion had watched her moving across the darkening lawns, her pale gossamer skirts lifting and settling about her feet as she came. A line of verse from his school days slipped unbidden into his mind: "Her feet beneath her petticoat, like little mice stole in and out as if they feared the light." He found it hard to equate this graceful, quiescent, almost somber-eyed girl, whose night-black hair floated long and loose about her shoulders, with the little virago who had given him such a hard time only a few hours ago.

He tossed away his cigar and stepped forward. She tensed but did not move, watching him warily.

"Good evening, Señorita Consuelo." His voice sounded deeper, more resonant out-of-doors, and it held a strong underlying vein of satire. "I trust you are recovered?"

"Recovered?" A small frown appeared.

"Lady Covington explained to the assembled company that you were indisposed," he said smoothly.

"Oh . . . yes. Thank you, I am better."

"I am pleased to hear it. Still, I am not sure that you should be out here alone—or were you perhaps hoping not to be alone for long?"

Consuelo said austerely, 'If you mean am I to have a secret assignation with Enrique, then I am not."

"I see. Perhaps that is why your young gallant spent the whole of dinner glowering at me!"

"You cannot expect him to love you!" she retorted swiftly, then, remembering her promise to Lady Covington, fell silent again.

There was an irrepressible quirk to his mouth, which vanished as he regarded her more closely. The light was going fast, but the little that remained caught a faint sheen across her cheekbones, an unnatural brightness in her eyes. So, she had been weeping.

The discovery moved him to pity rather more than he would have expected. He had not given much thought to her situation, and if she had figured in his mind at all, it had been as a tiresome spoiled child putting everyone to a great deal of trouble. He still regarded her as that but supposed that her predicament was deserving of some sympathy.

Nick had not met the hated Don Miguel but had a pretty fair idea of what he would be like, and was sure that compared to that young tulip of fashion with whom she fancied herself in love he must inevitably figure very much as the villain of the piece. Still, he had no wish to involve himself in debating the rights and wrongs of a young girl's foolish infatuations. The Spanish were notoriously hidebound in such matters. His task was simply to get her home.

Nevertheless, his manner toward her was more conciliatory as he said, "Lady Covington tells me that I have been clumsy in my dealings with you. If that is so, then I am sorry."

Consuelo threw him a swift, incredulous look.

"Not," he added, lest she mistake him, "that it changes anything. I meant every word I said earlier. However, I could perhaps have expressed myself more tactfully."

Her shoulders sagged perceptibly as the thread of hope vanished. She said in a very contained way, "It matters little how it is said. The message is the same."

"Perhaps if Lord Linton were to go in person to your father, he might listen?"

She looked steadily up at him. "Do you think it?"

"No, señorita," he admitted. "I fear it would be of little use."

"That is honest, at least." Her shoulders lifted. "What is to be, will be."

It sounded very much like an admission of defeat. Nick felt a pang of regret as he bent to pick up his coat, which lay folded on the grass. "I had better rejoin the dinner guests," he said without enthusiasm. "One can only stretch the smoking of a cigar so far."

"You do not care for Lady Covington's guests?" Consuelo asked provocatively.

"They are very well, I daresay, but drawing-room chitchat holds little appeal for me, I fear." He shrugged himself into the coat and tied his cravat into a careless knot. I did not come here to socialize." He looked down at her. "Will you walk back with me?"

"No," she said, too quickly. "Thank you, señor, but I do not care to go inside, either. There is so little time left to me, after all."

He hesitated, realized there was nothing more he could say and turned to leave. "Then I will bid you good night," he said abruptly.

"Señor . . ."

He had taken only a few steps when she called after him.

"Señorita?" He half turned.

"Is my father very ill?"

The question surprised Nick almost as much as the uncertainty with which it was uttered. He walked back and put a hand under her chin, feeling the resistance as he forced it up. "You are thinking of what I said?" She signified assent. "Well I will not conceal from you that I was concerned to see him looking so frail, but then we had not met for some months. Perhaps you would not notice so great a change." There was something in her eyes which made him say a little roughly, "Do not distress yourself, señorita. Your safe return will serve him as well as any physic."

Chapter 4

The black depression that descended upon Consuelo following her encounter with Captain Bannion lasted through most of the night. Guilt, that most insidious of emotions, wracked her constantly as she weighed her own happiness against the price of her father's health—perhaps even his life. And when she did drift into sleep, the specter of Don Miguel awaited her, unleashing the terror that something in his expression had evoked, terror she had pushed deliberately to the back of her mind for two whole years.

It was not fair, she reflected bitterly, that this thing should have come to her, that she should be shown what true happiness could be only to have it snatched away from her. Better, perhaps, if she had never come to England, had never known a freedom she would never have been permitted to know in Spain. Small wonder that after the initial strangeness had worn off, her natural spirit, for so long oppressed and subjugated by rigid conformity, had burst forth with such joyous abandon.

The Covingtons had been so very kind to her; also, she had met Enrique, who was everything she had ever dreamed about, as fair and handsome and full of romantic notions as any girl could wish for! How was

she to give him up—and with him, all that she had
come to value?

"I do not think I *can* return to what I used to be,"
she told her haggard image as she sat disconsolately
before her dressing mirror in the first glorious flush
of sunrise. "And, what is more, if my father truly
loved me, he would not demand so immense a
sacrifice!"

She would write to him again, explain to him what
it was that he asked of her, tell him how greatly she
had changed and beg him to release her from her
obligation.

But in case he should prove obdurate, she would
go through with the elopement as planned; after all,
Lady Covington would not have suggested it had she
not thought it expedient, and besides, it would be
the most splendid adventure!

Thus, her gloom was banished and she fell to decid-
ing how she could best pass the time until breakfast.
A ride would be pleasant. It was very early and there
would be no one about. A pity that she had not
arranged with Enrique last evening for them to ride
together. Still, it would be pleasant to be alone for
once, and if she was quick to dress, she could be
gone before Maria arrived to make objections..

In the stables there was only Stubbins, the head
groom, and a gangling lad who stood, apparently
transfixed by the sight of her, until Stubbins admon-
ished him for "gawping like a loony!" and told him to
put a lady's saddle on the little mare, Cherry—"not
as I think you should be going out alone, señorita,
beggin' your pardon, for I've only that great lunk,
Sam, to send along of you and small use he'd be if
you was needing help!" He sniffed. "Best you should
wait until one of the gen'lemen is about."

Consuelo's trill of laughter made nonsense of his

fears. "I am a very good horsewoman," she told him. "And besides, I shall not go far, Señor Stubbins."

The head groom knew that she was cutting him a fine old wheedle, but his misgivings were not proof against the missy's persuasive, melting black eyes. He gave up and shouted for Sam to bring the cob along for himself.

She truly had not meant to go far, but it was such a beautiful morning, with the air as fresh and pure as wine. Before many minutes had passed, it seemed, they had reached the little gate leading from Lord Covington's land out on to the downs. She signaled to Sam to open it for her with so much authority that the boy obeyed.

Soon they were high above the sea, with the sky, still faintly tinged with pink, looking newly washed where it met the deeper blue of the ocean, and a glimpse here and there of cliffs showing chalk-white against the turf. Below, in the distance, sunlight glinted on the onion-shaped domes of the Prince's splendid pavilion.

The fresh salt breeze coming off the sea was invigorating, and there was not a soul in sight. The temptation was irresistible.

"Come, Sam," she cried. "I will race you." And with that, she was away, galloping across the turf, leaving the boy on the cob hopelessly outdistanced.

As he struggled on gamely he heard other hoof-beats coming behind him. Lord Covington's new young hunter flashed past him, but it was not his lordship up in the saddle; nor yet Lord Linton, he realized, staring after the fast-vanishing figure. He urged the cob to an ambling canter, but soon even this proved too energetic for the beast.

Consuelo, too, heard the thunder of hooves behind her; unable to believe that it could be Sam, she glanced back and saw a horseman closing with her fast. Her reaction was spontaneous. She urged her own mount on ever-faster, until the little mare's feet scarcely seemed to touch ground and she was filled with a fierce exhilaration.

The pure fresh air after her sleepless night was like wine on an empty stomach. She was an eagle soaring, a beautiful ship running before the wind . . . skimming the waves. She laughed aloud, and the sound was dragged far away behind her to become a distant sigh.

The thunderous pounding grew louder, and she turned to see the hunter's head, nostrils dilated, neck muscles distended with effort. It drew level, and with dismay she saw that the rider was Captain Bannion, his blue eys, like ice chippings, narrowed in anger.

Panic drove Consuelo to urge the little mare further into headlong flight.

"Enough, Consuelo!" His words were caught and tossed away by the wind.

They were running almost knee to knee now, and when she showed no sign of conceding, he appeared to stand in the stirrups and, leaning across, arm outstretched, seized her bridle. For timeless moments they hurtled onward until she was sure that the sweating flanks of the two horses must collide. And then they were slowing, stopping.

At first neither could speak. Then she faced him, deeply ashamed but unwilling to admit it. Every limb trembled uncontrollably, every breath was an agony.

"How dare you do that!" she gasped. "No one has ever done such a thing to me!"

"Well, now someone has." his voice rasped as the air hit his own heaving lungs. "And it's not all I ought to do! Good God! Do you have the least idea how such behavior must appear? Racing across the downs like a hoyden, without escort, without any thought for appearances?"

"I had Sam . . ."

"A half-witted boy who could do no more than trail way behind you!"

"It would not have been so had you not come in pursuit. I had not intended to go so far."

"Do you say so?" He sneered. "You knew then who it was on your heels?"

"Not at that moment, no. But—"

"But you made a race of it, nonetheless. I could have been anyone—a total stranger! Pretty behavior, I must say, for the gently reared daughter of a gentleman! You should thank heaven that you are your father's daughter, señorita. Were you anyone else, I would take my crop to you as you deserve!"

"*Madre de Dios!* But you are insolent!"

She tried to wrench the rein from his clasp, but he would not relinquish it. Instead he slid easily from the saddle and slapped his hunter on the rump to send it ambling off.

"Come down," he ordered. "Give that poor animal a rest. She's earned it, goodness knows."

But Consuelo was by now quite as angry as he. She stared fixedly ahead. "Thank you," she said imperiously, "but I prefer to return home at once."

For answer he released the bridle, removed her foot from the stirrup and grasped her firmly around the waist, swinging her clearly and cleanly from the saddle. Her leg muscles quivered and almost gave way beneath her, yet when he seemed reluctant to let her go, her temper flared anew.

"Release me—*immediatamente!*" she demanded.

He complied, so abruptly that she staggered, and his eyes mocked her cruelly.

Consuelo summoned all her strength and dealt him a ringing slap. The contact between her gauntleted hand and his face was satisfyingly solid, so much so that it jarred her wrist to the bone.

He was momentarily disconcerted—but only momentarily. A red mark was already beginning to show on his cheek as he seized the offending hand in a viselike grip. Only then did Consuelo begin to have grave misgivings about the wisdom of her actions. There was a rather unpleasant smile in his eyes as, with his free hand, he closed her fingers into a tight fist, folding her thumb neatly over.

"There," he said with the soft vehemence that made her so uneasy. "That is the way of it if you wish to hit someone. Much more effective!" He paused and his voice softened still further. "Only don't try it on me again, my dear Señorita Consuelo, or by God you will get back more that you bargained for!"

"O-oh!" She snatched her hand away, angry, impotent tears blocking her throat and blurring her vision. "You are cruel, Captain Bannion!" she gasped. "An illmannered brutish person, as hard and unfeeling as . . . as . . ." She stumbled over the words and, looking wildly about her for a comparison, flung out an arm. "As those cliffs!"

But he would not be drawn further. "Perhaps I am," he agreed sternly. "But I am also the man your father appointed to act in his place, señorita. You would do well in future to remember that."

"If my father had known how you *really* were, he would not have entrusted you with such a mission."

"On the contrary, my dear, I suspect that it is precisely because he knows me so well that he desired me to go for him. No"—he held up a hand—"we will have done with this argument, if you please. It will get us nowhere." A new hardness entered his voice. "You might care to know that last evening I was almost brought to the point of feeling sorry for you, but my sympathy was clearly misplaced. This latest piece of mischief would seem to indicate that you do not merit so much consideration. I can therefore see little point in delaying our departure. And so I mean to tell Lady Covington that our plans are changed. We shall leave today."

Consuelo felt a great hollow in her chest. *What had she done?* Through her own thoughtlessness she had put her whole future in jeopardy. Lady Covington would be very angry, she was sure, to have all her careful plans set at nought. And rightly so, for she had gone to a great deal of trouble on their behalf. And Enrique . . . how would he regard her behavior? Perhaps he would assume that she did not care!

"Ah, no! Wait!" The captain had already turned away to collect the horses. She ran after him, stumbling over the grass in her urgency. "Señor Bannion, please listen to me!" Reaching him, she grasped his arm, not caring that she might lose face, not caring for anything but a need to make him change his mind. For that she would go down on her knees if necessary.

"What I did was very bad. I can see that! But it was not deliberately so. . . ."

His profile was unyielding. Without hurry, he looped the reins over his arms and turned to look down at her with a discouraging frown. But she would not be discouraged. His face blurred before her eyes.

"It was only that I did not think! Ah, Señor Bannion, I beg of you, do not take me away sooner than you must from this place that I love! I wonder do you have the least idea how my life had been until I came here?"

"Really, I fail to see . . ."

She plunged on. "You have met Señora Diaz . . . well, for the past three years, since the death of my dear Sancha who had been my duenna for as long as I can remember, Señora Diaz has been almost the only company I have had. Father entertained little, and when he did, it was for the business." Consuelo blinked away the stupid tears, impatient to see if her words were having the least effect. But his expression was impossible to read. "You have a high regard for my father, I know. And rightly so," she added hastily lest he think her undutiful. "He is a fine man. But as a parent, you see, he is not easy."

"The señor is most solicitous for your welfare."

The captain's words were a reproach which she met with unconscious irony. "Ah, yes. Also he provides most generously for my needs, and you must not think me ungrateful if I say that he would probably do as much for anyone placed in his care. But if he loves me, he has never expressed it . . . indeed, I sometimes suspect that only in his business dealings is he truly at ease. Even my betrothal was prompted by expediency. Have you met Don Miguel?"

He looked surprised. "No, but I fail to see . . ."

"He is almost as old as my father, and has buried two wives, and he has a son one year older than me—but you see, he is a very important client! And he wanted me . . . and my not inconsiderable dowry."

For the life of her, Consuelo could not keep the tremble from her voice. Her hands were clenched, her throat ached with the effort of holding back her tears, but she had almost finished and she desperately wanted to be taken seriously.

"What I am trying to say, Señor Bannion, and

saying very badly, I fear, is that not once has my father consulted me about what *I* want!" She swung away from him to face the sea as her voice finally cracked. "Perhaps you think me selfish to desire even that courtesy, but can you wonder that I envy your English young ladies their greater freedom? Or that I occasionally behave as—what was it you called me—as a hoyden?"

Nick Bannion watched the rigid, straight-backed figure, clenched fists held stiffly at her sides, and found his anger evaporating, for this was no spoiled child railing against parental authority, but a surprisingly articulate young woman deeply conscious of the very real social injustices in her life.

He was enough of a realist to recognize the truth of what she said. His own brief contacts with his mother's family had demonstrated to him how protective Spanish parents were of their girl children. He had heard tell of daughters living like cloistered nuns until their marriage. And should such a girl be so unwise as to flout the parental will in the choice of a husband, or if a father did not wish to provide sufficient dowry to attract an offer for her hand, a convent was often her fate—shut away forever from life.

Until now, Nick had not given such practices serious thought. He had known Señor Vasquez for several years and had always found him to be a courteous host and, a scrupulously honest businessman in all his dealings. Yet it had to be acknowledged that there was a reserve in his manner, a certain unyielding quality in his nature, that bore out all that Consuelo had said. So how would Vasquez, proud man that he was, react in the face of outright rebellion by his daughter? If he could not force her to the altar, might he not condemn her to eke out her days in a nunnery? He wondered if Consuelo had consid-

ered the possibility—and rather thought that with
her mind filled with infatuation for Henry Linton she
had not. There seemed little point in adding to her
distress. As it was, much as he might sympathize, he
had given his word to Señor Vasquez and there was
no way he could break that word. He paid Consuelo
the compliment of telling her so with complete
honesty.

"But I will do everything in my power to persuade
your father to heed your entreaties," he said, not
ungently. She turned to meet his eyes, and he gave
her a wry smile. "He just might listen."

"You are very good." She sighed. "But I do not
think he will."

At this moment the mare, which had been standing patiently behind Nick, came forward to nuzzle
her, and in spite of her misery, Consulo laughed. It
was a slightly hiccuping sound, but it lit up her face
quite enchantingly.

"I think she is wanting her breakfast," she said,
reaching up to run a hand lovingly down the mare's
neck.

"She isn't the only one," said Nick with a grin.
"Come along. Time to go."

As he helped her into the saddle she said, almost
diffidently, "Do you still mean to leave today?"

He tucked her foot into the stirrup with elaborate
care. "I wonder how soon I should come to regret it,
were I to be charitable?" he mused equivocally.

"You have decided to relent. I know it!" Consuelo
cried joyfully. "Oh, thank you, señor!" She cast him
a considering, sidelong glance. "And if you could also
not mention to Lady Covington—or anyone—about
this morning?"

He laughed aloud. "You, my child, are a minx! But
a persuasive one, withal."

They rode home in a surprisingly companionable fashion, with Sam, whom they had found still waiting on the patient cob, bringing up the rear, and Consuelo managed to gain her room without being discovered. Their state of amity continued throughout the day, earning Consuelo more than one approving, if curious, glance from Lady Covington.

The effect upon Lord Linton, however, was less salutary—indeed, once or twice he was almost short with her.

"But, *querido*," she explained. "I am only doing as I was asked."

"I don't recall Verena asking you to be so deuced pleasant to the fellow," he said stiffly. "I don't see, either, why she had to invite him to go about with us."

"I should think *that* is obvious! Lady Covington is simply trying to keep Captain Bannion happy so that he will suspect nothing." Consuelo put away the sudden unexpected qualm that assailed her. Perhaps the captain did not deserve to be served with such a trick after the kindness he had shown her earlier, but when one was fighting for one's only chance of happiness, such squeamishness was not permissible. She forced a laugh to her lips.

"Surely it cannot be that you are jealous, mi Enrique?"

But he would not respond to her teasing. Perhaps it was the heaviness of the day that made him so out-of-reason cross. The sun had vanished behind a sultry haze soon after midday, which was a pity for they had been invited to a Venetian breakfast, laid out with a sumptuous disregard for expense, in the huge conservatory of Madame Garrishe's charming Palladian villa at Ditchling.

Madame Garrishe was a lady for whom Consuelo

had developed a great affection. She was small, with quick birdlike movements and an ease of manner that made her comfortable to be with—the kind of woman Consuela liked to imagine her mother would have been.

There were so many people, friends and acquaintances, to be greeted that it was some time before Madame was free to talk. When Consuelo found her at last in the small saloon just beyond the conservatory, she was seated upon a sofa in one corner talking to Captain Bannion, of all people. He was very much at his ease, perched upon the window seat and conversing with surprising animation.

Consuelo would have withdrawn, but Madame had seen her. She smiled and beckoned her over.

"Consuelo, my dear child," she said in her light lilting voice, which held only the merest trace of an accent. "Do come and sit here beside me. I have been enjoying such an interesting talk with Captain Bannion. What do you think? I find that I knew his father rather well—when we were both a great deal younger, of course!" She chuckled. "I scarcely like to remember how long ago *that* was!"

"You need not worry, ma'am," said Nick with a lazy grin. "The years sit more lightly on you than they do upon him."

"Such gallantry!" Madame sighed, but she was pleased nonetheless. "I have not seen Sir Patrick in a long time now, but I would say that you are very like him in some ways. Such a handsome man he was, and as for charm—ah, *that* he had in abundance! It rescued him from many a scrape."

"And still does," said Nick dryly. "It seems to me that he spends most of his days one step ahead of the duns."

"Well, you are clearly not like your father in that

respect," she said, eyeing him with every show of gratification. "How enterprising, to make so interesting a life for yourself."

"Self-preservation, madame." He grinned. "I should go mad with boredom leading the kind of life enjoyed by my father!"

Consuelo had been listening with consuming interest. Did Madame truly consider Captain Bannion handsome? She turned a critical, slightly incredulous gaze upon him. One must allow that when his eyes crinkled up into laughter it added considerably to his looks. But handsome? He was altogether too . . . rough-hewn and careless of his appearance to meet with her approval, and besides, his brows were too black and heavy. No, she could not think him handsome, not when compared with Enrique. . . . She became aware that he was eyeing her quizzically, and a delicate blush ran up under her skin. She was relieved when Madame claimed his attention once more.

"And your mother's family . . . do you keep contact with them?"

"Very little. I visit occasionally when I have business in Valencia, but they are too pious for my taste."

The captain's tone discouraged further comment and Madame tactfully turned her attention to Consuelo. "Well now, my dear child. Tell me what you mean to do with yourself. Something more energetic than I would contemplate, I vow. You must not think yourself obliged to stay here with me, you know."

Consuelo was aware that Captain Bannion was awaiting her reply with quite as much interest as Madame. She said carelessly that she had hoped to explore the woods a little. "Only I think that Enrique finds the weather rather too hot, so it is not yet decided."

"I thought young Linton was looking a trifle

flushed," said the captain, with what Consuelo could only consider a want of sympathy. "I had assumed my presence to be the cause, but if it is the heat . . ." He shrugged. "No stamina, these town beaux."

Madame looked askance at them both and, seeing Consuelo's mulish expression, said placatingly, "Well, you look delightfully cool, dear child, in your pretty muslin dress. But then I daresay you are accustomed to the heat." She patted Consuelo's clasped hands. "I understand you are to return home quite soon now. I am going to miss you quite dreadfully."

Consuelo's glance flickered to Madame, to Captain Bannion, whose expression gave nothing away, and then down to her own clenched hands. "I, too, shall miss you, dear Madame," she said in a stifled voice.

"Never mind. You must write to tell me how you go on."

At this point Lady Covington drifted into the room, raised her eyebrows a little to see Captain Bannion so obviously on good terms with Madame Garrishe, smiled sweetly at Consuelo and said that Lord Linton had been looking everywhere for her. "I believe he means to take you walking in the garden. Ah, here he is now. Henry, did you not speak of taking Consuelo into the garden?"

Lord Linton seemed far from happy. He was perspiring freely, the points of his collar appeared to be more than usually constraining, and his cravat showed distinct signs of limpness. But good manners forbade that he should deny Lady Covington's words, and his beloved determined that he should not be given the opportunity.

Consuelo jumped to her feet before he had a chance to speak and professed herself quite ready to go.

"Put on your bonnet, child," called Lady Covington as they left the room. Her trill of laughter followed them. "What it is to be young! No thought for anything beyond the pleasure of the moment!"

Madame looked pensive. "Is it quite wise, my dear, to encourage Consuelo to be so much in Lord Linton's company when she is already betrothed? Anyone with half an eye can see how things are developing."

"I could not agree more, ma'am," said Nick Bannion grimly.

Verena Covington made a little moue. "Oh come! What a pair of killjoys you are, to be sure. The poor child must come to heel soon enough. Let her enjoy what is left of her freedom!"

This Consuelo was only too ready to do, but Lord Linton could find very little pleasure in the prospect of going out-of-doors and was having to be coaxed every inch of the way.

"It will be cooler under the trees, you will see," Consuelo told him. "And in the woods we may more readily discuss our plans."

But by the time they had crossed the garden and entered the wood, the sky had taken on a yellowish hue, and even beneath the trees the air was stifling.

"There will be a storm before long," Henry said with the air of one foretelling doom. "We'd have done better to stay indoors. See, everyone is turning back."

But Consuelo would have none of it. She clung to his arm, urging him on. She was slightly aggrieved that he did not wish to be alone with her and determined to tease him back into humor.

"Well, we will show them that we are not so poor-spirited, *querido*," she declared enthusiastically. "I shall not mind in the least if it thunders, so you need not concern yourself for me. In fact," she continued, anxious to relieve his mind of the necessity to shield her, "I am particularly fond of storms. The more violent they are, the more I enjoy them!"

Her words did not seem to be having the desired effect. There were times, Henry reflected with pardonable disloyalty, when Consuelo's wholeheartedness could be distinctly trying; at such moments, he was even brought to question the wisdom of the step he was contemplating, and was obliged to remind himself that Consuelo was in general a delightful girl—with an exceedingly wealthy parent—and that there were not many such who did not display far more distressing traits than mere high spirits . . . upon which marriage would hopefully exercise a sobering effect. . . .

"Enrique, you are not attending!" Consuelo's voice was plaintive. "I thought that you would be pleased to be alone with me."

"Sorry, my angel," he said, forcing himself to respond to her mood. "I am an unfeeling beast!"

She clung to him, immediately forgiving. "I think it is excessively romantic to be here—just the two of us." Her smile curved provocatively. "If you wish to kiss me, no one will see."

He did so and found her mouth sweetly inviting. But a distant rumble of thunder echoed across the sky, discouraging further dalliance. He drew away reluctantly. "Come—we had better get back."

"Oh no!" Consuelo was tugging at his arm. "See. Here is a most interesting path. Do let us explore it further. There may be somewhere we can shelter together. Only consider how much more romantic that would be!"

Henry stared in dismay. The path in question was little more than a rough track that disappeared almost at once into a dense thicket. He shuddered, contemplating the ruinous effect that unseen brambles would wreak upon his spotless unmentionables.

"Sweetheart, pray be sensible!" he urged. "The Lord only knows where a track like that might end."

"That is all part of the romance," she insisted.

"Well, I'm sorry, but it don't strike me that way. Not when the sky is growing darker by the minute."

"Oh, *basta ya*!" she exclaimed. "You are not at all amusing today!" And before he could prevent her, she had darted away from him and disappeared from view.

"Consuelo, come back at once! Do you hear me, you crazy little madcap? Come back . . ." Fastidiously he picked his way along the path and heard a trill of laughter somewhere ahead of him. As he had feared, brambles reached out at every turn to pluck at his clothes. He fended them off with mounting alarm and irritation. "Dammit Consuelo! This isn't the time for games. Where are you?"

"Find me!"

Her voice seemed tantalizingly close to his ear. There was a faint rustling to his right, and as he turned toward it the thunder growled nearer.

"There! What did I tell you? Oh, look, if you persist in this folly, we shall both get soaked to the skin!"

This time there was no reply. In the uncanny silence even the birds had stopped singing. Henry's annoyance turned to alarm. Suppose she had suffered an accident and was even now lying unconscious. It could take him hours to find her! The thought galvanized him into action. He must go for help. Another prolonged rumble of thunder decided him and he waited no longer.

He was almost in sight of the house when he came upon Verena and Captain Bannion hurrying toward the house. Very much aware of his disheveled appearance, he launched into a breathless explanation.

"Oh, the vexatious child!" Verena exclaimed. "However came you to let her do such a thing? Now I suppose we must search out one of the gardeners who will know his way about."

"That is precisely what I thought," said Henry in injured tones. "I was on my way to do so."

The first large spots of rain splattered down as Nick Bannion glanced from one to the other. "And in the meantime?"

They stared back in some surprise.

"It may take some time to find one of the gardeners. I think someone should go back now to try if they can find her."

"What the devil do you think I've been doing?" Henry exclaimed, affronted by the note of censure in the captain's voice. He indicated the state of his dress. "You could spend hours floundering around in that tangle of overgrown briars without finding anyone!"

"Then it's a pity you allowed the señorita to explore it in the first place."

"My dear captain, how disapproving you sound!" Verena Covington's voice held a trace of archness. "But you do not know Consuelo as we do. You may depend upon it, the child will only be funning. I shall own myself very much surprised if she is not at this very moment on her way back."

"I hope you may be right, ma'am. But if she is not?" A brilliant flash followed almost at once by a thunderclap added point to his question. "We will not waste time in surmising, if you please. My lord, if you will direct me to the path you spoke of, you may then go in search of your gardener."

Henry did not miss the note of derision but had

little choice other than to comply. He then ostentatiously offered his arm to Verena, who was equally annoyed at having a very promising interlude cut short. The gesture was wasted, however, as Nick was already hurrying away.

The black clouds were rolling up fast, and as he plunged into the depths of the wood the rain was already beginning a noisy assault upon the branches above him. He began to run, calling Consuelo's name and pausing to listen for anything resembling a cry. At last, above the now-constant crackle of thunder and the unremitting tattoo of the rain, he heard a faint answer.

"I am here! Oh, please to hurry!"

There was a note of desperation in her voice, or so it seemed to him as he fought his way through the head-high thicket to find her at last, a furious prisoner caught up in a patch of briars.

"Ah, Señor Bannion, it is you! *Madre de Dios* . . . I have been calling until I am hoarse!" A sob escaped her, born, he guessed, more of angry frustration than fear. "But where is Enrique? Oh, it does not matter. You can see how it is . . . I have tried and tried to free myself, and it only grows worse!"

His relief at finding her uninjured made Nick curt. "Stand still," he ordered, as he slowly and painstakingly freed her dress, which was fast growing sodden with the rain. At last she was able to step clear.

"Ugh! I am scratched all to pieces!" she cried.

"And so you deserve, my girl! Of all the stupid, ill-judged, irresponsible tricks to play . . ."

"You know nothing about it!" she rejoined, gratitude forgotten. "I did not ask for you to come. It was Enrique who was to find me!"

"Then you should have primed him better, my dear child, for clearly you don't know your man! Your precious Enrique is at this moment enlisting the services of a gardener to do his searching for him." Nick's voice was grimly scathing. "Very gallant!"

"Oh." Consuelo was deflated, but only for a moment. "Well, I expect he had good reason . . ."

"I expect he had!" They were both shouting above the noise around them, so that his sarcasm went unnoticed. "Now—do you think we might finish this discussion in more congenial surroundings?"

"I am sure I have no wish to remain here one moment longer!" cried Consuela, very much on her dignity.

The sight of that bedraggled figure striving to look imperious was too much for Nick. His impatience melted away and he began to laugh.

"*Insensato!*" she cried, turning upon him in a fury of indignation until, with the muslin flapping damply against her legs, she suddenly realizied what a comic figure she must cut. "Oh!" she wailed tragically, looking down at herself and then up at him. Then she, too, saw the funny side, and against a mounting crescendo of crashing thunder punctuated by stabs of lightning, they both laughed helplessly, holding hands until at last Nick took off his coat and pulled it tight about her shoulders.

A hissing zigzag of lightning struck nearby, bringing a tree crashing to the ground. Consuelo screamed and clung to him.

"Come along," he shouted, taking her hand and starting to run. "This isn't the time or place for an argument!"

Chapter 5

It had been very much feared that Consuelo would suffer a severe inflammation of the lungs as a result of her soaking in spite of being immediately wrapped in towels and rubbed briskly, then helped into one of Madame's gowns while her own was washed and pressed.

It soon became evident, however, that she was not the kind to succumb to any such weakness; not only did she remain outrageously healthy but was heard to remark a shade defiantly that she had found the whole adventure excessively enjoyable.

Nevertheless, she could not but be aware of Lady Covington's coolness toward her despite the fact that the incident had left her on much better terms with Captain Bannion. Henry had also been much put out by the afternoon's events, but with more cause, since his own role in them did not redound very much to his credit. It took much cajoling and self-abasement on Consuelo's part to coax him back into humor— which she set herself cheerfully to do, knowing full well that she had been much at fault.

"It was very bad of me, *querido*, to tease you as I did," she told him placatingly. "I would not have blamed you if you had left me to my fate instead of

63

rushing so nobly to find help. It was a great pity that Captain Bannion found me first, for I would much rather have been rescued by you."

The generosity of this admission went some way toward mollifying him and a visit to the theater in the evening accomplished the rest.

For Consuelo such a visit was still very much of a novelty. The theater in New Street was not a large building, but it was handsomely proportioned and fitted out with every regard for comfort; and filled as it now was with beautiful bejeweled people, all laughing and talking, it had an undefinable air of magic.

There were two complete tiers of boxes much ornamented with gold-fringed draperies that had been built to accommodate the more genteel members of the audience; the Prince's own box, more opulent than the rest, was separated by a richly gilded latticework screen.

The Regent was presented that evening, and after acknowledging the greetings of the audience, he made a special point of bowing to Lady Covington and her party, who were placed almost opposite his box. During the first interval he sent his secretary, Colonel MacMahon, to invite them to visit him. Consuelo did not like the colonel; she thought him an ugly little man with the strangest manners and a way of looking at her that reminded her of Don Miguel and made her feel hot and ill at ease.

The Regent, on the other hand, she liked enormously. He was extremely gross and splendidly dressed, and always greeted her with the most kindly twinkling smile.

"And how is my little señorita this evening?" he inquired, her hands swallowed up in his plump ones as he raised her from a deep curtsy. "In excellent looks, I see," he added archly. "Some little bird has whispered to me that you are to leave us very soon—to be married, eh? And who is the fortunate gentleman to be, I wonder?" A sly glance at Lord Linton accompanied this last.

Consuelo, acutely embarrassed at the thought of telling even a small lie to so noble a gentleman, hardly knew how to answer, but Lady Covington came smoothly to her rescue, explained the circumstances and begged leave to present Captain Bannion.

The Prince, well versed in all matters pertaining to the recent Peninsular Wars, was quick to link the captain's name with certain deeds of daring and was most complimentary. Captain Bannion, at his most urbane, conversed with him for several minutes and afterward remarked, with an ironical lift of one black eyebrow, that the Prince's knowledge of certain battles was so comprehensive that one might be forgiven for supposing him to have had a hand in winning them!

Lord Linton saw this as outright calumny against the throne and would have taken the matter further had Lady Covington not intervened to keep the peace.

It was later that same evening that final arrangements were made for the elopement. Captain Bannion had elected to go to the billiard room with Lord Covington upon their return from the theater, thus enabling the others to repair to her ladyship's boudoir without arousing comment.

"All must be decided tonight," Lady Covington insisted. "Tomorrow the house will be filled with people and it will be quite impossible to talk. Henry, I assume you have done your part?"

He gave her a pained look. "My dear Verena, I hope I am as capable as anyone of arranging matters! In fact, nothing could have been simpler. Green is to have my curricle ready to leave by four o'clock. He will not bring it to the house; I have instructed him to wait just beyond the first bend in the drive. There will be so many carriages about that one more will occasion little comment.

Consuelo had been feeling a little cast down, but now all her earlier enthusiasm returned. Her eyes sparkled with anticipation as they followed Henry's restless pacing. "It will be the most splendid adventure! And I have decided it is better that I tell Maria nothing. I can manage very well without her. My costume, *querido*—did you get that also from Green?"

"I have it safe in my keeping for now," said Lady Covington firmly.

"May I see it? Should I not try it on to be sure that it fits?"

"Later, child. When Henry has left us. And then you must retire, for there will be very little sleep for you tomorrow night."

The day of Lady Covingon's ball dawned clear, with the air much fresher after the storm. The house was astir from an early hour as the preparations of the past two days reached their climax. Already the ballroom chandeliers had been taken down and their lusters of finest Waterford crystal washed and burnished to a gleaming brilliance; now they were carefully rehung, and the floor was polished until it, too, shone mirror bright.

Then came the gardeners and footmen in an endless procession, bearing potted palms and ferns and fresh flowers to be arranged in great banks about all the principal rooms. In the kitchen an air of ordered frenzy prevailed as the chef de cuisine and his minions labored to create all manner of delicacies guaranteed to tempt even the most jaded palate.

It was not the first ball Lady Covington had given

during Consuelo's stay, but the young girl never tired of watching all the preliminaries. After the sheltered life she had led, the transformation of the main rooms seemed magical, like something from another world.

The thought of so many people still had the power to reduce her to shyness, but her confidence was growing daily, and most of Lady Covington's friends were very kind to her. Nevertheless, it was comforting to know that Madame Garrishe would be there and that she was to stay overnight.

It would be nice to see Madame just once more before she left. Consuelo hoped that she would not think too badly of her when her elopement with Enrique was discovered. It would have been comforting to confide in Madame and seek her approval, but no—Lady Covington had been quite adamant that no one should know.

More than thirty people sat down to the dinner preceding the ball, for many of Lady Covington's friends were residing in Brighton for the summer months. Nick Bannion had hoped to excuse himself from the festivities, but such retiring ways found no favor with his hostess.

"I will not hear of it, my dear sir." Her husky voice was reproachful. "How can you even suggest such a thing? No—I will allow of no excuse," she continued as he pleaded a lack of formal evening wear. "Of course, you did not expect that you would need it, but my brother's clothes should fit you, for you are much of a size. The closet in his room is amply supplied and I am persuaded that were he here, he would be the first to make you free of whatever you need."

Nick could protest no further without being made to appear ungracious. He must be grateful, he supposed upon inspection of the aforementioned closet, that the absent peer's tastes ran to plain well-cut coats—a circumstance which enabled him to present himself at the appointed hour in black long-tailed evening coat, black knee breeches and a discreet white waistcoat.

Madame Garrishe, coming upon him in the rose drawing room where the guests had foregathered to await dinner, thought him by far the most attractive and interesting of Verena Covington's would-be conquests, for there was little doubt in Madame's mind that it was not for Consuelo's sake that Verena had set herself to charm the captain. He was that rare animal among present company—a real man rather than a mere fashionable fribble.

Sitting with him at dinner, she said, "Our little Consuelo is looking particularly well this evening, is she not?"

Nick glanced along the table; it was not the first time his eyes had been drawn to watch Consuelo this evening since the moment she had come into the drawing room in her beautiful dress. The dress had tiny puffed sleeves, a deep neckline trimmed with creamy lace, which looked so well against her pale olive skin and flattered her slight figure, and a skirt that fell in soft folds to a lace-trimmed hem. She appeared, he thought, as coolly regal as any princess with her shining hair piled high in a cluster of curls, her head proudly carried; as he watched she turned aside to listen to something Lord Linton said to her and her profile was exquisite.

"The señorita is a constant enigma," he reflected aloud, causing Madame to look at him curiously. "Her moods change like quicksilver. Which is the real Consuelo, I wonder. Do you know, Madame?"

"Ah! I might, Captain, but I am not sure that I

should enlighten you." She gave him a droll look, which made him smile. "We women, you see, must treasure our little stratagems; to reveal all would be to lose our mystery! However,"—she grew more serious—"there can be little doubt, I think, that our little one is much troubled at present though she hides it well."

Nick felt the implied criticism. His voice grated a little. "No one can be more aware of that fact than I, believe me! My position is a damnable one. Would that I had not allowed Lady Covington to sway my judgment, for it seems to me now that this prolonged stay of sentence, as it were, only makes matters worse."

Madame Garrishe was a little surprised by his vehemence. It emboldened her to say diffidently, "Well then? Is there no way Consuelo might be permitted to remain?"

At once the line of his jaw hardened. "Regrettably, Madame, the decision is not for me to make."

There seemed little more to be said, and Madame Garrishe skillfully turned the talk to less contentious matters. And indeed, as the evening progressed and the ball got under way, it seemed that she might have been overly pessimistic, for Consuelo appeared to be enjoying herself prodigiously.

She endeared herself to all and was never wanting for a partner, moving from one dance to the next with seemingly boundless energy.

"Would that one were seventeen again!" Verena Covington sighed with a light laugh that barely concealed her vexation.

Nick looked down at her with a gleam of amusement. His eyes lingered appreciatively over her gown of palest green satin, which revealed rather more than it concealed.

"Surely not?" He murmured with the audacity of a man very sure of his ground. "Only consider the disadvantages of being seventeen—how limited your pleasures would be, how stifling the obligation to conform!"

She laughed, well pleased with his impudence. "You have a fine, backhanded way with a compliment, sirrah!"

"You must blame the life I lead. The sea is a demanding mistress, more so than any woman I have yet met. She deals in harsh reality, so that one quickly grows impatient of mere flummery." His smile was mocking. "There is nothing quite like a spell at sea for bringing out the best, or worst, in a man"— his smile broadened—"or woman!"

"Really? My dear captain, you interest me greatly!" Verena swayed tantalizingly closer, her breath quickening. "I wonder what such a test would tell you of me?"

If she had thought to discompose him, she was quite out. He cast a swift glance around the ballroom where a quadrille was in progress. The couples engaged in the dance were absorbed by the intricacies of the steps, and those not dancing were equally preoccupied in watching those who were, or each other. Lord Covington had left to await the arrival of the Regent.

The temptation to play her ladyship's own game was almost irresistible. Nick looked quizzically into the green eyes, made more brilliantly alluring than usual by the happy positioning of a spray of emeralds in her red-gold hair, which caught the light with every turn of her head.

"What indeed?" he murmured. "There are, of course, other, more pleasurable ways of discovering those little intimate details of character. . . ."

She responded exactly as he had supposed, her tongue flicking pinkly against pearly teeth, her voice at its huskiest as she hazarded a guess as to what he had in mind.

His grin was quizzical to the point of provocation. "Ah, as to that, my lady, so delicate an exchange can only be conducted in the utmost privacy"—he glanced up—"and I fear we are about to be interrupted."

Verena could have screamed with vexation as she followed his glance and observed Lord Cowley approaching. She had determined that Captain Bannion should partner her in the next waltz; whether he performed well or not, she neither knew nor cared, so long as she could feel his arms about her.

By the time Lord Cowley reached her side, however, she had her emotions firmly under control and was smiling. Her introductions proved superfluous as the notable exquisite turned a patrician countenance toward the captain, his voice droll.

"Nick Bannion, so it is you! When I marked your presence at dinner, I could not at first believe it to be possible." He raised an eyebrow at his hostess. "My dear Verena, how *did* you manage to lure the intrepid captain from his beloved ship for even a brief respite?"

"Then you know one another?"

"Cowley and I were at school together," Nick offered dryly, and saw that she was reassessing him in the light of this information.

"Really? How extraordinary!"

"Yes, isn't it?" His lordship sighed. "Our paths have seldom crossed since, of course, though one hears of Nick's exploits from time to time." He ran long slim fingers down the black riband of his quizzing glass. One eyebrow lifted delicately as he surveyed the companion of his school days. "Can this be the man who avowed that he would rather by far stride his quarterdeck—or whatever it is that sailors do—than grace a drawing room?"

"It depends on the drawing room," Nick drawled, acknowledging his hostess. "But you need not fear that I shall ever seek to rival *you*, Vernon. I know my limitations!" He glanced across the room to where people were beginning to drift together for the waltz. "I wonder, would you both excuse me?" He bowed and strode purposefully away.

Verena said nothing, but Lord Cowley heard the sharply indrawn breath and was curious. He turned to find her watching Nick as he advanced upon a group of young people with Señorita Vasquez at its center.

"Dear me!" he said in his droll way. "Forgive me—did I spoil sport?"

"Don't be ridiculous, Vernon!" she snapped, but the spots of color high on each cheekbone belied her denial. Her chagrin was in no way diminished as she presently watched the captain leading Consuelo onto the floor.

Consuelo had been taken aback when Captain Bannion had expressed a wish to dance with her, the more so as she observed the determination with which he overcame the good-natured objections of her companions in order to achieve his object.

"Are you enjoying your ball?" he asked as he whirled her expertly about the room.

"Thank you, yes." It was shyly said, for his closeness confused her and the dance was making her breathless. To be sure, the captain did not have as light a touch or move with Enrique's grace, but there was an exhilaration, a vitality in the way he waltzed, a disturbing sureness in the way he held one.

"You are certainly very popular," he observed dryly.

"It required a great deal of persistence on my part to secure this dance with you."

She glanced up at him pensively through her lashes, and his face—eyes laughing, his teeth a blur of white—seemed to dip and swirl, darkly etched against the shimmering lights. "I did not suppose that you would wish to do so."

"Not wish to dance with the most beautiful young lady in the room? For shame, señorita!" His voice, softly teasing, disturbed her. "You may have cast me as the villain, but even a villain must be granted an occasional boon!"

She could feel a warmth stealing into her face and knew that her embarrassment was due as much to guilt as any other cause. If he could but know what a trick she was about to serve him, how different would be his manner. But a swift recollection of what was at stake stiffened her resolve. She could not allow any qualms of conscience to sway her now.

Nevertheles she felt obliged to say in fairness: "You are not so bad! Indeed, you have shown a tolerance greater than I had any cause to expect and I would like to . . . to thank you!"

It was a halting little speech and she hoped devoutly that he would attribute her difficulties to breathlessness or nerves, or both. To her relief, this seemed to be the case—at any rate, he seemed no more than surprised and mildly amused.

Soon afterward the Prince Regent arrived with his party. As usual he had insisted in his genial way that no ceremony be attached to his presence at the ball; Lord Covington had a saloon set aside as a card room, and as soon as his royal highness expressed himself ready, he would be escorted thither. But for some little while he remained in the ballroom, conversing amiably with all who approached him.

Once more he singled out Consuelo, beckoning her to come to him. She made her deepest curtsy, which delighted him. He was heard to regret lustily that he was not a few years younger—and slimmer! "For it would then have been my privilege to claim your hand for a dance, my dear little señorita. I was thought to dance prodigiously well in my day! Is that not a fact, Lady Covington?" His twinkling eyes sought hers.

She smiled back dutifully, not altogether pleased to be chosen as His Royal Highness's contemporary.

"But alas, that day is long past." He sighed, unwittingly compounding his felony.

"Then the matter is simple, Prince," Consuelo told him with one of her roguish glances. "If you wish it, you may have the very next dance and I will sit with you instead of dancing."

He laughed heartily at this and allowed himself to be led to a nearby sofa where he would have an excellent view of the floor, where sets for a quadrille were forming.

"Who is this child who commands royalty thus?" murmured Lord Cowley, taking up a place beside Madame Garrishe. "Why have I not seen her until now?"

"Señorita Vasquez is visitor to our shores—and a most charming one. We shall miss her greatly when she returns home—as she is shortly to do—for she is something of an original, is she not, Captain Bannion?"

"She is certainly full of surprises," Nick agreed, watching the vivacious little figure so patently at ease with her magnificently appareled companion.

Chapter 6

As the night wore on, Consuelo's unremitting energy was the object of much envy and some speculation. She was very gay throughout supper, though in fact she ate very little; it was, thought Madame Garrishe, as though she were seeking to cram into the few hours that remained to her as much pleasure as was possible.

It was something of a surprise, therefore, when Madame came upon her at last sitting alone in one of the anterooms beyond the ballroom. She looked pale and all eyes, prompting Madame to inquire anxiously if she were perfectly well.

"Oh, yes." Her wan smile seemed to refute the assertion. "It is only that I wished to be quiet for a few moments."

Madame sat down beside her and patted Consuelo's clasped hands reassuringly. "It has been a very long evening, my dear, and you have scarcely been off your feet in all of that time. I am sure that it would be no small wonder if you were now quite exhausted!"

"Oh, no! That is not why . . ." Consuelo's color deepened a little. She seemed loath to explain; in fact, her manner was altogether rather strange. Madame Garrishe was curious but made no attempt to press her. Presently Consuelo moved restively and asked in a carefully casual way, "Do you think, Madame, that if there is a—a decision made which affects one's whole future happiness, that one should hold to that decision despite the qualms which may assail one?"

Something in the way she spoke made the old lady feel uneasy, but as she was fearful of prying too far and perhaps frightening away any further confidences, she only said lightly, "Dear me! What a very profound question for so late an hour! It very much depends upon the nature of any such decision. Are you perhaps," she hazarded tentatively, "troubling yourself about the betrothal that your father has contracted on your behalf?"

Consuelo started, recovered herself and said rather confusedly that it was something like that.

"Well, then, my dear child, if I were you, I would put all such doubts out of my head. It may seem to you to be a very strange way to go about things, but some of the most satisfactory marriages have been arranged in this way." She was choosing her words with care, not wishing to distress the child by mentioning Lord Linton by name. "My own was just such a case. I had bestowed my affections elsewhere and quite thought my life at an end when Papa demanded that I give Jules up and marry Monsieur Garrishe. But, of course, it was not so! Such passions seldom last and monsieur and I lived together most agreeably for many years."

Consuelo turned slowly and subjected her to an intensely searching look. "But, forgive me, Madame, but did you *love* your husband?"

Oh, dear; how foolish it had been to delve into matters that did not concern one! Madame reproached herself in vain. "I grew very fond of him," she said firmly. "There are, after all, many degrees of love—some, like exotic blooms, are not destined to survive."

"And what happened to your Jules?" Consuelo persisted .

There was an infinitesimal pause and a small involuntary sigh. "He went away."

For some reason Consuelo did not react at all in the way Madame had expected. Gone was the subdued, indecisive girl; it was as though whatever had been troubling her was suddenly resolved, and she was her own buoyant self again.

"Thank you, Madame!" she exclaimed enthusiastically. "I now know exactly what I must do."

Madame Garrishe was not sure for what she was being thanked, but was relieved that her words seemed to have had the desired result. On the point of getting up, Consuelo leaned forward in her impulsive way to hug the old lady and press a kiss to her cheek.

"In case we do not meet again," she said tremulously, "I want you to know that I shall miss you more than almost anyone! But I shall write to you, if I may, and I hope that you will remember me with sufficient fondness to write also to me!"

"Oh, my dear!" murmured the old lady, enfolding her in a tender embrace. "I, too, shall miss you; and of course I will write! It would grieve me very much to lose touch with you."

For a moment they clung together, and then Madame put Consuelo gently from her, seeing the girl's overbright eyes through the blur of her own tears. "Come now; we are being very silly! And I shall see you again before you leave, for I am staying here tonight, or had you forgot?"

She was saved from a reply by a sound near the

door. Henry came in, relief evident in his fair handsome face.

"So this is where you are, Consuelo. Verena and I have been looking high and low for you!"

"Well, you cannot have searched very far, Enrique, for I have been here all the time with Madame Garrishe." She gave a great sigh, released her friend's hand with a smile and stood up. "And now I believe I should like to dance again," she said gaily.

Henry took her arm and shot her a meaningful glance. "It is almost two o'clock, my dear. Don't you think . . . ?"

"But I am not in the least tired! Just one dance, Enrique, and *then* I will think."

Lady Covington was at the far end of the ballroom when Henry led Consuelo out onto the floor. She frowned and moved toward them as quickly as she could without apparent haste, but as several people detained her along the way and the music had already begun, she was obliged to watch as they performed their part in a lively country dance. The crowd had by now thinned considerably, but those who remained, mostly younger people, were still enjoying themselves prodigiously.

"That child should be in bed." Nick Bannion's voice behind her was severe and made her jump. "She will scarcely be fit to travel at this rate."

Verena had suffered a frustrating evening at Captain Bannion's hands. There had been no mistaking his interest in her—at times it had been quite markedly provocative—yet he had proved elusive at every turn. She knew not whether this was deliberate on his part, but it was not what she was used to. Never before had she encountered the least difficulty in bringing to her side any gentleman who took her fancy, and the captain's behavior—whether intentional or not—piqued her.

It showed in her voice as she said with a touch of asperity, "Surely, Captain, you will not deny Consuelo and Lord Linton these last moments of happiness?"

He was quizzical, his eyes straying from hers to watch the graceful figures at that moment performing a lighthearted *tour de main.* "Isn't that being a trifle melodramatic? From what is, I admit, a brief acquaintance, I would hazard that the señorita at least is possessed of far more resilience than you give her credit for!"

"Well, of course she is!" Verena's laugh a trifle shrill, her bruised spirits exacerbated by hearing a note almost of admiration in his voice. "I am sure that no one can seriously suppose that Consuelo's heart will be irrevocably broken when she leaves here! But even so . . ."

"Ah, there you are, m'dear!"

Lord Covington's jovial voice boomed in their ears. His wife drew in a sharp little breath.

"And you, too, Bannion; that's splendid, splendid! I've just seen old Prinny off . . . he spoke most kindly of you, sir . . . enjoyed his game of picquet with you, y'know. Said it was a treat to have a new set of brains to pit his wits against. His lordship chuckled. "Ye damned near beat him, by Jove!"

Nick grinned. "Damned near! But that would hardly have been polite, would it?"

"What? Ah, I see . . . . quite so, sir. Enough said!" His lordship cast an indulgent eye over the dancers as the music drew to a close. "Now there's a pretty sight, wouldn't you say? Pity. A great pity." He sighed. "Still, I hope we've succeeded in making your stay an agreeable one at least, Captain Bannion?" He glanced slyly at his wife.

"Most pleasant, I thank you, sir," Nick said equably.

"Captain Bannion is a little concerned that Consuelo will be overtired, my love, so—ah, there you are, my dears." Verena was all sympathetic concern as the young couple came toward them, laughing, swinging hands. "Consuelo, my dear child, I really do think it is time you retired. You have a long day before you, and Captain Bannion has been so accommodating that I feel we should make every effort to abide by his wishes now."

Consuelo was obliged to veil her eyes during this speech to hide their mischievous sparkle, and so looked suitably acquiescent. By the time she came to make her good nights, she was able to achieve a convincing air of subdued gravity, which affected Lord Covington so much that he was obliged to blow his nose very loudly after his "dear little puss" had reached up impulsively to kiss his cheek.

She was aware that Captain Bannion was watching her intently, and this fact alone was enough to arouse her mettle. She was proudly erect, a little tragic, as she bade him good night and turned away with Henry, who had been permitted to walk with her to the stairs. Lord Covington mopped his eyes as he watched her go, and Verena called out that she had a little something for her.

"I will come to you shortly, my love!"

Safe in her room at last, the confused emotions of the past few hours found their release in a sudden rush of tears. This came as no surprise to Maria, who had been expecting something of the kind. The only surprise was that it hadn't come sooner, what with half-packed portmanteaux and bandboxes lying about the room for the past two days and Señora Diaz overseeing it all in an ill-omened silence like a flat black crow.

Consuelo quickly pulled herself together, however, and submitted to being undressed with no more than a brief, regretful glance at the beautiful dress as it was folded to await packing.

She sat meekly before the mirror as Maria unpinned her hair and brushed it until it shone before tying it back in a ribbon. When all was done, she dismissed the maid—clinging to her for a moment with sudden fervor, her eyes big and dark with emotion.

"You need not worry about me anymore, Maria," she said in a choked voice. "I promise you, I am quite resigned to what must be. Oh, and you are to wake me at eight o'clock."

"But señorita, I thought . . ."

"It is arranged," said Consuelo firmly. "Eight o'clock."

When the maid had gone, she prowled about the room in her nightgown, unable to settle anywhere for more than a moment. It would be necessary to write a note exonerating Maria, she thought, and did so swiftly, signing her name with a flourish—the last time, she realized with a feeling of awe, that she would sign anything as Consuelo Beatrice Dominica Vasquez. When she left this place, it would be to start a new life and if . . . when she returned, it would be as Lady Linton!

There came a faint scratching on the door and her heart leaped. But it was only Lady Covington. She was carrying the carpetbag containing Green's suit and his hat.

"Now then, you know what you are to do," she began without preamble, setting it down on the bed. "I am still not sure that it would not have been better to have your maid privy to the secret. If you should fall asleep . . ."

"Dear Lady Covington, I shall not sleep; *I could not sleep*. And see, I have my little watch here so that I shall know exactly when to creep down the back stairs to meet Enrique." Consuelo put up her head. "You can trust me to play my part, I promise you!"

"Good." Lady Covington nodded, satisfied. "Well, I had better get back to my guests. There are still a few who have not yet left or retired to their rooms. I must speed them on their way! And besides . . ." She half turned, and the pale green satin showed quite clearly the line of her thigh. She stood admiring the effect in the mirror for a moment before continuing complacently, "I have promised to show Captain Bannion the terrace by moonlight before he leaves." She smiled. "After all, the later he retires, the more likely he is to sleep soundly!"

"Yes. That is very clever of you." Consuelo held out her hands. "Then I must bid you farewell, dear lady, and thank you for all that you have done for me."

"My love." Lady Covington pressed a cool cheek to Consuelo's and stepped away. "I hope all goes well with you. If so, we should meet again very soon."

As soon as the door had closed, Consuelo tipped the contents of the carpetbag out onto the bed and, unable to wait a moment longer, wriggled out of her nightgown and was soon dressed in shirt and breeches, a colorful kerchief tied at her neck.

"You make a very fine boy, I think," she told her reflection with some pride, preening this way and that. And it was true that her slight figure lent itself perfectly to the groom's clothes, "But your hair will not do like that, *amigo*."

She rummaged feverishly among the piles of bag-

gage for Maria's sewing box and, finding it, extracted
a pair of scissors.

"I do not know how well I may achieve this, but
. . ." With a frown of deep concentration, tongue
pensively caught between her teeth, she clipped and
sawed her way through her beautiful hair, struggling
to reach the very back of it, and resolutely banishing
the pangs of loss she felt as the rich silken tresses fell
one by one to the floor. "What is the sacrifice of a
few hanks of hair, after all, when compared with the
possible success or failure of so great a venture!" she
rebuked herself severely. "And besides, it will soon
grow again; very soon!"

She was in part consoled by the results of her
impetuous actions, for the figure looking back at her
in the mirror had now assumed a truly masculine air.
She turned her head experimentally, and the bobbed
hair, in spite of its somewhat ragged ends, clung
neatly to her head. It was like looking at a stranger.
She rather thought Enrique would be angry at what
she had done, but it was too late for repining. She
pulled Green's hat well down and hoped that the
brim would hide her handiwork for the present.

Her watch told her that it was almost time to go.
She put on the jacket and quickly collected her toilet
necessities and the sprigged muslin dress she had
decided to take with her, cramming them carelessly
into the carpetbag. Then she took a last look around
the room, picked up the watch and pinned it to her
shirt inside the jacket, then quietly opened the door.

Chapter 7

Downstairs all was still. Consuelo found her way to the side door without difficulty and slipped out. Light still blazed from the ballroom windows, and she saw faint shapes moving about as the servants began to extinguish the candles one by one.

"Are you there, Enrique?" she called very softly. There was a footfall behind her and she swung around with a soundless gasp. "Oh, it *is* you, *querido*! Just for one moment I thought . . ."

"Quiet!" Henry commanded edgily. He took her bag and put a hand under her arm. "If we follow this path along the shadow of the yew hedge, it will take us on to the main drive. Green is waiting with the curricle just beyond that clump of trees."

The night was soft, the sky clear, velvet-black and glittering with stars. Somewhere close by the gardeners had been scything the grass, and its earthy, pungent sweetness still lingered on the air. Up toward the terrace someone called a name and there was laughter, fading away.

Henry felt her stiffen and said, low-voiced, "It's all right—still one or two people about, but it don't signify. If we should be seen, we'll be taken for guests making a belated departure."

Beyond the bend of the drive was the curricle, with Green striving to contain the restless horses.

"They don't take kindly to being kept standing, guv," he grumbled. "Not when they're as fresh as these beauties!" He peered, frowning at Consuelo, not by any means approving of this latest quirk of his master's. Women was usually trouble in his book, notwithstanding that this Spanish señorita was a taking little piece—light as a bird, too, judging by the ease with which his lordship lifted her into the curricle.

"Oh, but you should have let me climb up for myself, mi Enrique," she protested with a giggle. "No one will take me for your groom if you have such a care for me!"

"Time enough for that later," he said, leaping up beside her and taking up the reins. "Right—let 'em go, Green."

But this proved too much for the groom. It was all very well her looking the part, which she did right enough, but "it ain't sense, guv, not taking me along! The young lady won't be a mort bit of use to you when it comes to blowing up for the tollgates or seeing the horses right, beggin' your pardon, miss . . ."

"Stop complaining, lad, and do as you're told!"

"But . . ."

Consuelo leaned down confidingly to him, her smile bewitching. "I know how you must feel, Green, but you see, it is essential that we go alone, for it will look most remarkable if Lord Linton has two grooms! Oh, and I must thank you for lending me your best suit. I will take the greatest care of it, I promise you!"

"Consuelo for pity's sake!" snapped the much-tried Henry. "Green—no more arguments if you value your job. Let 'em go!"

Acknowledging defeat, Green complied with a

suddeness that took everyone by surprise, including the horses. But after a momentary indecision they took the bit, and the carriage flashed past him to be swallowed up in the darkness.

Consuelo maintained a discreet silence for some time, sensing that Enrique would have his hands full while the horses were so fresh. Now that they were actually on their way she felt a kind of exhilaration. She had never before traveled at such a pace in the darkness, but when she ventured to say so, Henry laughed and told her that this was not fast. As her eyes adjusted she became aware of just how many things she could distinguish—trees from hedges, walls that ended in high white gateposts, and as they passed through Brighton, the dark mass of houses. . . . Then they were out into the country once more and going at a steady pace.

"Dawn will be breaking before long," Henry said. "I want to put as many miles between us and Covington Manor as I can before daylight. There's a turnpike coming up—hand me the yard of tin, will you?"

"Oh, may I do it, Enrique?"

Before he could dissuade her she had the horn to her mouth and blew a mighty blast.

Henry laughed. "We'll make a tiger of you yet," he said as they left the tollgate behind, and the horses were let out once more. "I shan't stop at Cuckfield; this team should be good as far as Hand Cross, I reckon."

"But surely there will be nothing to fear for some time?"

"All the more reason to press on as fast as we can," said Henry grimly. "Bannion's no flat, and he's going to be as mad as fire when he discovers that you've given him the slip. I don't care to meet up with him if I can avoid it!"

Consuelo felt the faint stirrings of unease. "Then we must hope that Lady Covington's ruse is successful." She told him what her ladyship had intended. To her surprise Henry laughed in a rather strange way. "I thought it quite clever of her," she insisted.

"If it works," said Henry derisively. "Which I doubt. Verena has been trying to fix her interest with the good captain these two days past to very little purpose! And even if she does succeed now, I can't see Bannion oversleeping when he has an important commission to fulfill, can you?" His voice sharpened. "Another turnpike ahead."

Consuelo blew up with less enthusiasm this time, her mind being occupied with something rather unpleasant, which she did not wish to have clarified but which would not be wholly dismissed. Finally she asked in a very casual way: "You said that Lady Covington wished to 'fix her interest' with Captain Bannion; what does this mean?"

Henry shot a quick look at her. The road they were traveling ran at present along a dense hollow between high hedges, but away to the left the first light of morning was paling the sky; it illumined a profile both youthful and proud. "My dearest Consuelo, can you really be such an innocent babe?" Her chin rose a fraction. "Why, yes. I believe you really are!" He shrugged. "Well, perhaps it is better that you remain so."

She turned dark eyes to him. "No," she said flatly. "I am not *so* innocent. It is simply that I . . . I did not wish to think of Lady Covington in that way. . . ."

His laugh held genuine amusement. "That is rich; by George, it is! My dear, you must have been going around with your eyes shut if you didn't twig it!"

A great feeling of pain was reflected in her eyes—

the distress of having one's idol torn down. "Yes, I must."

"Oh, look, Consuelo, I'm sorry. I thought you knew. That kind of intrigue is the breath of life to Verena, and Bannion presented more of a challenge than most since, though he looked, he didn't fall like a ripe plum the way most men do." Her sharp little intake of breath made him say crossly, "Well, why else do you suppose we have been kicking our heels for the past two days?"

"It was because of the ball." But she said it without conviction.

"It was because Verena needed time to bring the captain to heel."

"And you think that she might have succeeded last night?" asked Consuelo in a small voice.

Henry shrugged. "I have never known her to fail with any man she really wanted."

There was a bleak little silence as Consuelo digested this. She wished very much that she had not succumbed to curiosity, for a train of thought once started was not so easy to stop. She wanted very much to ask if he had been one of her conquests, but feared that he would put into words the suspicion that now plagued her, for had he not been one of Lady Covington's most assiduous escorts when they had first met?

She said instead: "Does Lord Covington know, do you suppose?"

"Look, Consuelo. Do we have to talk about Verena's affairs?" Henry said irritably.

"No, of course not." She sighed and pulled herself together. It was of no use to repine over something that was past; after all, if her Enrique had once cherished a tendre for Lady Covington—and it would not be remarkable if he had, for she was very beautiful—at least it was herself that he now loved and wished to marry. She said, much more cheerfully, "You are right, *querido*, for I would much rather talk about us!"

This she proceeded to do quite happily and without any need for participation on his part for some considerable time. By the time they had passed through Cuckfield, the sun was up and shedding a thin golden radiance across the misty undulating countryside. Soon they were crossing Staplefield Common and climbing the hill toward Hand Cross.

Consuelo, looking about her, was much struck by the beauty of the vale through which they had just passed and which now lay spread out behind them; little roads wound through copses and here and there among the trees she glimpsed a snug red rooftop. England was such a lovely green country, she decided—something that even a scorching summer could not destroy.

When Henry saw what the Red Lion in Hand Cross had to offer, he wished that he had changed horses in Cuckfield, but it was clear that his team could go no farther, so he made the best of what was available and arranged for the safe return of his horses to Covington Manor.

"Do you want breakfast?" he asked Consuelo in tones that made it clear that he would very much begrudge the delay. So she obligingly stifled a yawn and her growing hunger pangs and assured him that she had not the least desire to eat.

They had not covered many miles, however, before Henry's worst fears were realized and he was cursing his luck in being landed with as poor a team of jobbers as it had ever been his misfortune to have in hand.

"Not an ounce of go in them," he fumed. "It is to be hoped we fare better next time!"

Consuelo sighed. This elopement was not at all how she had imagined it would be. Those first few miles in the darkness had been the very stuff of romance, but more and more now Enrique was becoming obsessed with his tiresome horses.

"How far did you say it was to this Gretna Green?"

"Some three hundred and sixty miles," said Henry without taking his eyes or his mind far from the road.

"And how far have we traveled?" Consuelo persisted.

He made a small irritable sound. "Oh, I don't know—about twenty miles, I suppose."

"*Madre de Dios!* But it will take us days!"

"Three days, perhaps. We haven't made bad time at all so far," said Henry huffily, defending the implied slur upon his driving. "And you knew from the start that it was a long way."

"Yes, but I had not then considered . . ."

"Well, if you don't want to go through with it, now is the time to say so," he snapped.

"When have I said that I did not wish it?" Consuelo cried, equally incensed. "You are putting into my mouth words that I have not said."

"Perhaps. But I have no wish to go tearing about the country on a wild-goose chase! I was under the impression that you were in love with me—but perhaps I was mistaken!" The whip whistled expertly out to point the leaders, urging them to greater effort.

Consuelo glanced at the grim, handsome profile and was horrified. In one more moment they would be quarreling in earnest and the fault was hers. "Ah, *querido*, forgive me! Of course I love you—*con toda mi alma*. You must not heed my silliness . . . it is only that I am impatient to arrive!"

If Henry accepted her apology with a poor grace, she did not notice. She was resolved to think before she spoke in the future and was several times obliged to bite on her tongue to curtail its propensity for inconsequential chatter.

At last the stoutly maintained silence penetrated Henry's guard; he glanced her way, and the sight of that grimly concentrating figure made him aware of his selfish preoccupation as harsh words never would have.

"I am sorry," he said with a rueful smile. "It was unfair to take out my aggravation on you. Look, we should be in Horley soon. We'll take breakfast there, and then we shall both feel much more the thing. What do you say?"

Her generous acceptance of this olive branch went a long way toward mending his ruffled feelings.

When they reached Horley they found the yard of the Chequers Inn well astir despite the earliness of the hour. A Brighton-bound coach stood ready for the off, its new team with postboys already mounted and eager to be away as the hurrying figure of a recalcitrant passenger was seen emerging from the inn doorway.

"Try and remember that you are my tiger and not my prospective bride," Henry adjured her as he secured the reins and leaped down, leaving her to dismount alone and kick her heels as he summoned a passing ostler and gave very definite instructions.

To while away the time Consuelo stepped inside, where she found a public room with a large table laid with a white cloth upon which a motley array of used dishes, cups and saucers, tankards and the like, lay scattered and for the most part abandoned. Only two gentlemen still sat over their tankards, indulging in a desultory conversation. At the end of the table near-

est to her was a plate of bread and butter, so enticing
a sight that, with the pink tip of her tongue already
licking speculatively at the corner of her mouth, she
wondered if she might take just one piece without
being noticed.

At that moment, however, one of the gentlemen
looked up and glared at her in such a way that she
retreated hastily and met Henry coming in. Enthusiastically she told him about the breakfast room. Henry
viewed it with distaste and turned away to summon
the landlord and demand a private room.

"I should not mind that other," Consuelo confided
in a whisper. "Only consider what an adventure it
would be!"

Henry quelled her with a look. "A fine spectacle I
should make were I to be discovered taking breakfast
in a communal room with my tiger for companion!"
he murmured as the landlord came to bow them into
a small pleasant room with dark furnishings. "Do try
to mind your behavior until we are alone! We want
no suspicions roused lest Bannion should come asking
questions later."

In consequence, Consuelo stood subserviently near
the doorway as a nubile young maidservant scurried
back and forth with delicious-smelling dishes of eggs
and ham, fresh bread and butter and a jug of ale.
Growing bold, the maidservant treated the young
tiger to a pert, inviting smile from under long lashes,
and Consuelo, entering into the spirit of the masquerade, winked at her.

When the door had closed behind the maidservant,
she giggled "Did you see that? I did very well, I
think!"

"A veritable boy," Henry agreed with a reluctant
grin. "Now you may come to the table."

Without conscious thought Consuelo removed her

hat and tossed it onto a chair, thus affording Henry his first real glimpse of of her shorn locks. His grin faded to a frown of dismay.

"Good God!" he ejaculated faintly. "You crazy girl; what have you done?"

Nick Bannion was up early, dousing his head with cold water to relieve the faint throbbing at his temples. His bag was packed and ready for a prompt start.

He would not, he decided, be sorry to leave. The sheer triviality of this kind of life, cocooned as it was by pleasure and wealth from the least hint of reality, held no lure for him. And though Verena Covington's charms were undeniable, there was something altogether too calculating, too predatory about her.

He preferred women of a more generous disposition—delightful, warm-hearted creatures who gave as freely as they took and asked nothing of him that he was not prepared to give. Verena Covington would never be satisfied until she had a man at her feet, and he knew that his unwillingness to play her little game only served to fan the flame of her desire. The sooner he was away, the better.

The whole of the west wing of the house lay under a blanket of silence as Nick left his room to make his way downstairs. It was to be hoped that Consuelo's maid would rouse her in good time and that the unzealous Señora Diaz would for once bestir herself.

Nick was almost down the first flight of stairs when a scream penetrated the silence above. Instinctively he turned, taking the stairs two at a time. Doors were beginning to open all along the landing as he ran past, while the scream, sustained with surprising vigor and with only the briefest of pauses for breath, made its source comparatively easy to locate.

He arrived on the scene to find the door of a

bedchamber flung wide and Señora Diaz—a pale, voluminous wrap clutched to her person and a bed cap of awesome ugliness framing her distorted features—half standing, half swooning against its solid frame. Out of sheer exhaustion her screams were rapidly diminishing to a series of hysterical, incoherent emissions as she stared wild-eyed into the room.

It required little intellect to deduce that the bedchamber was Consuelo's or that he would find it empty; nevertheless, he pushed past the duenna to discover for himself what was the reason for so violent an outburst. He found the maid, Maria, also in tears as she crouched on the floor in front of the dressing table over something which at first he took to be a discarded garment of black silk.

Only when he stooped to touch it did he discover it to be hair—great, raggedly cut swaths of Consuelo's beautiful hair. He gathered up a handful and was shaken by a wave of anger at the desecration of something so exquisite.

He stood up to find that a small crowd had gathered in the doorway in a motley array of night attire, ranging from the exotic frogged dressing gown of Lord Cowley to the snowy-white folds of Madame Garrishe's robe; all were agog to know the cause of the fuss.

Before he could speak, however, the crowd parted to admit Lady Covington, in a floating peignoir of palest pink. She appeared, as always, unruffled.

"Why, Señora Diaz, whatever is wrong?" She stepped past the hysterical duenna without waiting for answer. "Captain Bannion, where is Consuelo?"

"Where indeed, ma'am?" Apart from a harsh little laugh, his voice was carefully expressionless, though his eyes blazed. He was, in fact, cursing himself for not foreseeing this turn of events. "I very much fear the bird has flown the coop."

"Flown?" She was admirably composed. "Why, whatever can you mean—flown?"

"I mean, ma'am, that Señorita Vasquez has gone—run away. And I shall own myself very much surprised if Linton is not also found to be missing."

"Gracious!" Verena Covington took the long switch of hair he still held, looked at it reflectively for a moment and then tossed it back with the rest. "Silly child," she said, and meeting his eyes: "As to Lord Linton, someone will, of course, be sent to his room at once, though I am sure you must be mistaken."

"Pray allow me that honor, ma'am," said Lord Cowley smoothly.

"The señora was most insistent that I should not wake her until eight o'clock," sobbed Maria. "I thought she would be angry that I had disobeyed!"

Señora Diaz uttered a shuddering moan and had to be helped to a chair. Someone suggested hartshorn and yet another burned feathers. In the end a vinaigrette was produced, and Lady Covington suggested with more than a trace of asperity that Maria should assist the duenna to her room, and reluctantly led the way herself.

With most of the excitement seemingly at an end, people began to drift back to their rooms, suddenly embarrassed at being caught en deshabille. Madame Garrishe, however, remained behind. She hugged her wrap to herself and looked troubled.

"Poor little Consuelo." She sighed, and as Nick turned with a frown, went on: "We spoke together in the early hours of the morning. She was in a very strange mood—low in spirits, you know?"

Nick stared. "Consuelo was?"

"Oh yes. It was not the face she showed to the

world, but . . ." Madame shrugged. "After we had talked and I had, as I thought, reconciled her to this marriage her papa arranged for her, she seemed quite elated once more. I realize now, of course, that when she said, 'I know exactly what I must do,' she was contemplating something quite different. I am sorry."

Nick gave her a small smile that was meant to reassure her. "You must not hold yourself in any way to blame, Madame. We have all been equally deceived."

"Shall you go after her?"

"I must," he said. "She is my responsibility. Fortunately there is only one direction they can have taken if they mean to marry."

"We cannot be certain, of course, that Lord Linton . . ."

"I am certain," Nick said harshly.

Madame looked at him with troubled eyes. "You will not be too hard on Consuelo, Captain? I am sure, thinking back to our conversation, that it was the idea of deceiving her friends that sat so ill with her."

He frowned in polite disbelief. "That's as maybe, ma'am . . ."

Lord Cowley put his head in at the door, the tassle of his magnificent cap swinging gently at his ear. "You were right, Nicholas, dear boy. Young Linton is likewise missing." He gave a droll little smile. "And now I suppose you will be obliged to set off in hot pursuit up the Great North Road. So fatiguing!"

Chapter 8

But there was much to do before Nick could set out anywhere—questions to be asked, arrangements to be set in hand—and though he lost no time about it, quite an hour was like to be wasted before he could leave.

It very soon became evident that the maid had played no part in the elopement—her shock and distress being in no way assumed—but Green was clearly hiding something.

The young tiger put up a brave show of innocence, but he was expecting Lord Covington to question him and had been confident of his ability to fool the amiable old codger; what he hadn't reckoned on was being interrogated by a grim-faced gent "as was well up to snuff when it came to dealing with raw young 'uns," and the truth was wheedled out of him in a matter of minutes.

Lord Covington was much distressed to learn that his little missy was running around the countryside got up like a groom, and was further shocked to know that Linton had condoned the masquerade. Without a moment's hesitation he offered Nick the pick of his stable to ride after them.

"Tell Stubbins to saddle Major, m'boy. He ain't

quite as showy as that new stallion, but he's got good bottom—carry you mile upon mile without flagging!"

Nick thanked him and promised that the horse would be safely returned. Lord Covington poohpoohed this, saying that all he hoped was that the captain might come up with the irresponsible pair before any harm was done.

Nick hastily finished the last of the breakfast that Lady Covington insisted he take before he left.

"If you are to be chasing all over the country, you must at least eat before you leave," she said a little peevishly. "Though for my part, I don't see the necessity. Why not let them go? Once they are married, Consuelo's father can do little about it, after all. Would that not be kinder to Consuelo in the long run?"

Nick pushed his plate away. "I did not come to be kind. I came to take Consuelo home, and that I mean to do."

"So sure of yourself, Captain?" she mocked.

"So sure," he agreed. He swallowed the rest of his coffee at a gulp and stood up, turning once more to Lord Covington. "And now, sir, if I might presume even further upon your kindness?"

Lord Covington assured him that he would do all that was in his power.

"My thanks. Then, if I might have pen and paper? I must send word to Mr. Fletcher, my first mate, explaining why we are delayed. Is there someone you could send? I will give you the direction. And, further to that"—he turned to Verena—"if you would try to calm that hysterical duenna so that she and the maid may be got to London dock by this evening. I will order a post chaise in Brighton."

"My dear sir, we would not hear of it, would we, my love?" Lord Covington looked for confirmation to his wife. "You must allow us to put our own traveling coach at their disposal."

Nick bowed. "You are more than kind, my lord." He turned to Verena once more and found her looking at him in the oddest way, her green eyes very wide, a slight flush on her cheek.

"So you do not come back here?"

"No, ma'am. We shall go straight to the docks." He engaged that glance with an ironical little smile. "I must thank you for making my stay so pleasant. I am only sorry that Consuelo's visit with you both has ended this way. No doubt she will write to you."

Verena shrugged and turned away almost rudely, leaving her husband to make her apologies.

"This affair has upset her, don't you know!" he blustered as she left the room.

Nick made good time on the road. His first piece of luck was at Horley, where the landlord recalled the gentleman well.

"Marked him special, I did sir, on account of how he was regular caring of that young tiger of his. Took him along of himself to partake of breakfast in my little back parlor there. It's a thing as you don't see happen often, sir."

"Quite so," Nick agreed, downing a pint of the landlord's best brew. "I believe his lordship has quite a fondness for the lad! How long ago would this be?"

The landlord scratched his head. "Well, now; he arrived just as the Brighton coach pulled out, so I reckon it must've been around nine when he left—in a proper fret he was to get on, he was! Seems he told Jeb out in the stable yard as he needed a strengthy, quick-actioned team as different as maybe from them bone setters as he was driving. There was some talk of a sick relative, I remember, someone as he had to reach before nightfall."

Nick set his tankard down on the table. "Thank you, landlord, you have been most helpful."

At Croyden he was less than two hours behind the fleeing couple and was just beginning to congratulate himself when he lost track of them completely. Several people remembered having seen a curricle very much like the one he described, but no one, it seemed, could agree upon the occupants of the equipage, and since none of those described bore the least resemblance to Lord Linton, he was reluctantly drawn to the conclusion that they had given him the slip.

As if this were not aggravation enough, he must now also face the possibility that Linton had taken Consuelo to London and not to the border as he had supposed; if so, it would be the devil's own work to find them.

It was this conclusion as much as any other that prompted him to hold to his instincts as it was his wont to do when in a tight corner; his intuition had served him well enough in the past, and intuition told him that the couple were headed for the border. Apart from other considerations, Linton would find it a well-nigh-impossible task to find anyone willing to marry them in London, and Nick hoped that he had read Consuelo's character well enough to be sure that she would settle for nothing less.

By the time he reached Welwyn he was hot and tired and so was the horse which had carried him nobly thus far. His inquiries drew a blank once more. At the White Hart he encountered a most appetizing smell coming from the regions of the kitchen; it proved to be a casserole of rabbit, a speciality for which landlord's wife was renowned. Nick needed little persuading to remain, for he discovered of a sudden that he was devilishly hungry.

It was when he was embarking upon his second helping of apple pie that sounds of raised voices began to penetrate the dining-room roor.

"I do not care, Enrique!" Consuelo's excitable tones were unmistakable. "I cannot go another mile without food!"

"Well, it will have to be something quick; that broken trace has already cost us valuable time!" Lord Linton sounded less than happy.

Nick was across to the door in seconds and had flung it wide.

"*Madre!*" said Consuelo blankly. "How are you here?"

"Never mind how." Nick eyed the trim little figure grimly, subduing a traitorous inclination to admire the way her boy's raiment became her. His glance lifted to encompass her hair, now hatless, and his cold rage returned in full measure.

Henry, who had gone to hail the landlord, returned from the taproom and halted in dismay on the threshold, a deep flush suffusing his face. "Deuce take it!" he muttered. "I knew this would happen!"

The landlord appeared at his elbow. Nick addressed him curtly. "A private room, if you please—and quickly!"

It was a voice that brooked no argument. Bursting with curiosity, the landlord begged them to follow him, and Henry, on the point of refusing, looked at Nick, shrugged and went along with a brave show of carelessness to the small parlor where he threw off his drab driving coat and flung it over one of the chairs before going to stand at the window. When the landlord had left the room, he began, "Now, look here . . ."

But Nick cut him short. "You will do better to remain silent, my lord, for there is little you can say to justify this day's work!"

Indignation got the better of caution. Henry stepped forward, a scowl marring his fair handsome features. "You are insolent, dammit!"

"Yes, you are!" Consuelo cried furiously, laying a protective hand on his arm. "Also, you are unjust. Enrique has done nothing of which he need to be ashamed. I came with him very willingly!"

Nick turned on her a look of withering derision which raked her from head to foot, making her for the first time very much aware of how revealing were her breeches.

"*Your* behavior, señorita, deplorable as it is, proves only that you are a silly irresponsible girl and in no way exonerates Lord Linton from blame, as he well knows!"

"*Madre de Dios!* You go too far, Captain! I will not permit you to speak so to me!"

His lip curled, but his eyes were like hard blue chips of ice. "Have a care, Consuelo," he said softly. "My friends would tell you I am not a tolerant man. Provoke me further and I will use more than harsh words, believe me. You have upset a great many people by this piece of work and have put me to a considerable amount of inconvenience. I tell you plainly, I am in no mood to be provoked!"

Painful tears were blocking Consuelo's throat so that she could not have defied him if she had wished to—and looking into those unrelenting eyes, she knew it would be a pointless exercise.

Nick saw that he had silenced her for the moment, though there was nothing submissive about those proud, glittering eyes. He said coldly, "I believe you have a dress with you? Your maid said there was one missing from your baggage. You will oblige me by changing into it at once. I will arrange for a room to be put at your disposal."

The two young people looked at one another, and for a moment the parlor air was charged with all kinds of undercurrents. Then Consuelo shook her head. It was an infinitesimal movement, but Lord Linton shrugged as though accepting the inevitable.

"Very well," she said in a flat little voice. "But I will have to fetch it."

"His lordship will oblige, I am sure." Nick stared pointedly at Henry, who strode to the door, tight-lipped. While he was gone, Nick called the landlord and made arrangements for Consuelo to change.

She heard him without really listening. Her finger drew absently around a large cabbage rose on the chintz cover of one of the chairs while her mind bent itself to devising some means of extricating herself and Enrique from this insupportable situation, which she saw as a setback rather than defeat. If only someone here in this hostelry could be persuaded to help . . . perhaps when she went to change into her dress? The churning of fresh hope inside her revived the pangs of hunger which had been temporarily eclipsed by more urgent considerations. But now pride was stronger even than the claims of her stomach, and pride would not permit her to ask Captain Bannion for anything—even food.

When Henry returned, she took the bag from him with a dignity that made her look oddly piquant in her boy's raiment, and touching his hand for a moment, she said softly, "Do not despair, *querido*."

The captain held the door for her, subjecting her to a close scrutiny as she passed. She returned his look with hauteur.

"Don't be long," he said briefly. "I have a post chaise ordered."

Consuelo followed a servant girl to a tiny bedchamber with a low sloping ceiling, and there she struggled out of the breeches and made full use of the ewer of water placed in readiness for her. "Ah, that is better!" She sighed, not altogether sorry to be rid of the groom's hot stuffy clothes. The dress of jonquil-colored muslin was cool to her skin and in place of her riding boots—which she had been obliged to wear because Green's shoes were much too large for her—she was able to don cotton stockings and her pretty yellow Roman sandals.

The young maid had watched and waited in an awed silence, which she broke to whisper, "Oh, miss, I wouldn't know you for the same person, straight I wouldn't!" And then, diffidently: "Will I put these . . . these garments into the bag, miss?"

"But yes, for they do not belong to me and, I suppose, must be returned, though I do not at present see how."

There was a small stand mirror on a table near the deep-set window, which stood wide open to the afternoon, and by perching on the end of the bed, Consuelo could see to brush back the damp tendrils of hair from her forehead. The rest of her hair was still a very ragged bob, which defied any tendency to curl. But perhaps soon it would not look *so* bad. She dismissed it with a resigned shrug and in the mirror saw the young maid's eyes big with unasked questions. With a conspiratorial grin she confided the whole of her adventure thus far, her enthusiasm sometimes leading her into the realms of fantasy.

"And so, you see, this cruel captain has come along to blight our love, and unless we can find a way to escape him I shall be forced into a life most miserable!"

The much-embellished tale appealed greatly to the impressionable young serving girl, whose life was starved of anything approaching such flights of romantic drama. "Oh, miss! Whatever will you do?"

The maid's soulful utterance was cut short by three long blasts on a horn, which announced the arrival of a coach in the yard below them. A bell rang in the stable and the yard was suddenly full of clamor. Consuelo ran to the open window and put her head out.

"Where is it bound? Do you know?" she demanded of the maid.

" 'Tis the northbound mail, miss."

Consuelo swung around, her eyes dancing. "Do you suppose . . . ? Oh, if I only had some money!"

There was so much unconscious yearning in her voice that the maid hesitated for no more time than it took to thrust her hand deep into her apron pocket. "Here, miss. It en't much, but it'll get you a goodly way along and then you'll maybe have something as you can sell."

Consuelo looked at the coins through a sudden mist of tears. She did not need anyone to tell her that their meager total in no way corresponded to the extent of the girl's sacrifice. "My thanks," she said huskily. "But I cannot take all your money."

"Oh, but you must! I . . . I shan't miss it, truly. Sometimes, folks is extra-generous, see . . ." The lie was convincingly told, but still Consuelo hesitated. "Look here, miss . . . I *want* for you to take the money! P'rhaps it'll bring you luck. Only there's no time to dither, see . . . the coach'll be away any minute now!"

"Very well, then, I will . . . and *thank you*!" Impul-

sively Consuelo flung her arms about the startled girl
and hugged her. Then she flew about the room,
collecting up her things and stuffing them willy-nilly
into the carpetbag. "Now . . . oh, what is your name?"

"Floss, if you please, miss."

"Floss? That is a pretty name. Well, Floss, can you
get me down the stairs without being seen? And
please to try if you can take Lord Linton—he is the
fair handsome gentlemen you will find in the parlour
below—on one side and tell him what I have done?
Madre de Dios—I must go!" Consuelo snatched up
the bag and, on an impulse, unpinned the tiny pearl
broach at her throat and pressed it into the maid's
hand. "There! It is of no great value, but it is
quite pretty, I think. No, no, take it! You can wear
it with your Sunday dress. And now"—she heaved
a sigh and grinned at her co-conspirator—"let us go,
quickly!"

When the parlour door had closed on Consuelo,
Henry had made to follow, but Nick barred his way.

"Where do you think you are going, my lord?"

Henry's face was a dull red. He was beginning to
feel decidedly ill used and wished devoutly that he
had never allowed Verena to talk him into this preposterous venture. Eloping might be all very well if
one were passionately in love, but though Consuelo
was a delightful girl, he was not at all sure that his
feelings for her were sufficient to sustain him in the
present circumstances. Nevertheless, he could not,
as a matter of honor, admit as much.

So he said stiffly, "If you must know, I am going to
find the landlord. I have no desire to stay in this
room with you, and besides I badly need a drink—
and something to eat!"

Nick eyed him sardonically. "Don't be a young fool. Sit down. I haven't nearly done with you yet. No, sit down!" he ordered as Henry prepared to ignore him; and as he saw the pugnacious thrust of the younger man's jaw: "Yes, I daresay you would very much like to send me to Jericho, but I don't advise you to try! And as for food, there is some ordered—it will be here at any minute—and I want to try to talk some sense into you before Consuelo comes back."

His tone had become less brusque, and after a moment Henry shrugged and turned back into the room.

"That's better." Nick watched as the young man walked across and flung himself down upon the window seat. His manner was ungracious, and so close to being childishly petulant that Nick said dryly, "Before I go any further, my lord, I beg you to believe that I find my present position every bit as damnable as you do yours. I set out, albeit reluctantly, to do a favor for a friend and find myself, instead, embroiled in a situation that is fast growing into something more nearly resembling a melodrama!"

"Then I don't see why you persist," muttered Henry. "You might well be considered to have done all that could be expected of you."

"Do you think so?" Nick's lip curled. "But then, you see, I don't like unfinished business—nor do I care to be so callously deceived. However, to come to the point, my lord: it is no part of my function to query your intentions where Consuela is concerned. . . ."

"Just as well, for I'm damned if I'd tell you!"

"Quite so. Nevertheless, it probably comes as no surprise to you to learn that Señor Vasquez is an exceedingly wealthy man?"

"That was not a consideration," said Henry quickly, but without conviction.

"I hope not," said Nick dryly. "Because if you imagine for one moment that the señor could ever be brought to forgive Consuelo the kind of elopement you are contemplating, or that he would think twice about cutting her out of his life in consequence as though she had never existed, then I must tell you that you are hopelessly out!"

Henry stood up suddenly as though unable to sit at ease one moment longer, and Nick knew that he had judged him aright. "You seem very sure?"

"I know my man. He has a totally inflexible set of precepts by which he lives and judges others, and these one ignores at one's peril. So your only hope of winning Consuelo is to go and put your case to the señor personally."

"Small use that will be, when this Don Miguel already has a prior claim!"

"That does rather complicate the issue, but surely it is worth a try? If Señor Vasquez has a weakness, it is that he is an ardent admirer of the English aristocracy! Your present title and future prospects must therefore be in your favor. If you can also assure him that you and Consuelo are deeply attached, that, together with the fact that you have chosen to act honorably, might well further dispose him favorably toward you." Nick paused to let the words sink in. "For what it is worth, I will add my voice to yours."

"You?" Henry stared, suspicious. "Why would you do a thing like that?"

The door opened to admit waiters bearing dishes of cold meats. Nick watched as they spread a cloth on the table near the window and set the dishes upon it. It occurred to him that Consuelo was being an unconscionably long time. When the waiters left, Henry repeated the question.

"Why not, my dear Linton? Strange as it may seem"—Nick was faintly amused—"I am not such a villain that I would see Consuelo condemned to abject misery for the rest of her life! And speaking of that young lady"—he strode to the door—"I'd better go and hurry her up. You make a start, if you've a mind to."

Left alone, Henry stood for a moment in thought. Did he really want to go traipsing all the way to Spain to eat humble pie to some haughty Spanish merchant? But an exceedingly rich merchant, he reminded himself. It was surely worthy of consideration.

He picked up a knife and began to carve a slice of ham. The door behind him opened and he turned, expecting that it would be Consuelo.

But it was a young serving wench, very ill at ease, very red in the face. She dipped a hasty curtsy, looked fearfully over her shoulder and whispered, "Could I have a word with your lordship, if you please, sir?"

Chapter 9

Consuelo, wedged between a stout lady with several bandboxes and a man whose coat reeked of ale and stale perspiration, found herself with ample time on her hands in which to reflect upon the possible consequences of her own impetuosity. Suppose that Floss could not intercept Henry to tell him what she had done? The money Floss had so generously given her had bought her a fare to a place called Stamford, and beyond that she could not think.

And what of Captain Bannion? She supposed that he might easily discover where she had gone if he were to question the ostlers at the inn. But it would not be wonderful if he had come to the end of his patience and decided to abandon her to her fate!

A deep depression settled on her spirits, which was not much relieved by a rakish-looking gentleman opposite her who ogled her constantly. She wished very much that she was still wearing her breeches, so that she might have passed unremarked.

The stout lady obviously disliked the man's attitude also, for she glared him out of countenance before turning with some difficulty, laden as she was, to face Consuelo. "On your own, are you, dearie?" She wheezed in a kindly protective way.

Consuelo nodded.

"Surprised at your family, letting you travel alone, I am." She glared once more at the man and lowered her voice dramatically. "You can't be too careful, mark my words!"

"No. I am sure that you are right, señora, but" —Consuelo improvised hastily—"you see, I have no family in England, and am on my way to . . . to friends at Stamford."

"Foreign, are you, then?"

Consuelo saw fresh interest gleam in the man's eyes and gave him her haughtiest look as she introduced herself to her companion.

"There now—Spanish! Fancy that! Well, I'm Mrs. Rudge, m'dear." The boxes were being juggled around most alarmingly on the plump knees until, finding the one she wanted, the lady managed to get it open. "What would you say now to a bite to eat, eh? There's some chicken legs wrapped in this napkin, here, and there's bread and some cheese." She puffed as she spoke. "And I've a pot of pickles somewheres about. . . ."

"Oh, thank you!" Faced by the sight of so much food, Consuelo's insides began to churn with expectancy. "If I might just have a leg of chicken?" she asked shyly.

"Lord love us, m'dear! You'll be wanting more than that! Take two . . . and one of these bread rolls. Made them myself this very morning, I did, and there should be some beef pasties . . . Well, look now, if they haven't got all squashed! Still"—a deep chuckle shook her—"they won't taste any the worse for that, I daresay."

The chicken legs, a pasty and two large slices of plum cake later, Consuelo thanked her companion and sat back with a sigh of satisfaction to watch in awed fascination as her benefactor ate steadily on. She was surprised to discover how much more optimistic one could feel on a full stomach.

The heat inside the coach made her drowsy. It seemed a very long time since she had first set out with Henry . . . was it only that morning? She must have dozed off, for she awoke to find some kind of commotion going on outside and the coach swaying crazily, so that, if she had not been packed in so tightly, she would have fallen.

"What is wrong?" she gasped, yawning.

"Well you might ask?" said Mrs. Rudge grimly. "It'll be one of them young scallywags up top—bribed the driver to let him tool the coach, you see if I'm not right! We'll be lucky if we don't overturn!"

The coach lurched once more.

"Gracious!"

The rakish gentleman who had been leaning out of the window now ducked back in again. "It would appear that you are right, ma'am. As far as I can make out, the fellow is engaging in a race with a curricle that is endeavoring to overtake us, and at this present rate, we are like to end in a ditch!"

There came a sharp compelling blast on a horn and the gentleman leaned quickly out the window again. "It's the curricle coming up fast; they're never going to try and take us with that bend ahead!" he cried in disbelief. "Yes, by George, they've done it! Oh, what a splendid effort—driven to an inch!"

The excitement over, the coach gradually returned to its normal pace. Everyone relaxed and Consuelo heaved a great sigh.

"How far have we come?"

"Well, m'dear, I don't properly know . . ."

"That last turnpike we passed through was about three miles short of Baldock," said the rakish gentleman, presuming upon recent events to pursue his interest with Consuelo. The boldness of his eyes made her feel hot. "You're to be met at Stamford, are you?"

"Yes," she said briefly.

"Quite a coincidence, that. I'm bound for Stamford also. Suppose your friends don't show up?" he pressed. "Not at all the thing, a pretty young woman like yourself stranded all alone in a strange town—in a strange country, too, by all accounts!"

For the first time she felt a lurch of fear; it must have communicated itself to Mrs. Rudge, for she patted her hand reassuringly. "That's none of your business, sir . . . and I'll thank you to remember it!"

He raised a derisory eyebrow but said no more as the other passengers were by now showing varying degrees of interest and concern. Consuelo answered their questions politely while the panic inside her grew. She began to wish . . . oh, she did not know what she wished, except . . .

There was a loud oath from the coach driver, joined by other voices, and the whole framework shuddered as the brake was hastily applied.

"Now what?" The rake sighed as, amid the pandemonium above, there was mention of something blocking the road ahead. He moved once more toward the door, but before he could reach it, it was wrenched open and a figure filled the aperture—a blessedly familiar figure.

"Mercy on us!" cried Mrs. Rudge.

"Captain Bannion!" Consuelo exclaimed faintly, quite disproportionately glad to see him.

"Señorita," he returned with an enigmatic lift of one black eyebrow. "This is the end of your journey, I believe?"

A babel of surprise, conjecture and eagerly proffered

advice ensued throughout the carriage while Consuelo sat, unable to move, her eyes locked with his.

Behind him the guard was in a belligerent mood. "This 'ere is most irregular, sir—the stopping of a public coach upon the King's highway without proper cause! And I must warn you that this weapon is loaded. . . ."

"Give me your bag, Consuelo," said Nick calmly.

She came out of her reverie and did so, preparing thereafter to squeeze herself out of the seat.

"You en't going with this person?" Mrs. Rudge eyed the interloper with deep suspicion—as swarthy-looking an individual as she'd clapped eyes on for many a day. "I really don't think you ought . . . At Stamford you said your friends was to meet you, and we en't anywhere near Stamford. . . ."

"Besides which, *respectable* folk don't go a-holding up coaches is what I say!" This from another of Consuelo's would-be protectors.

"Oh, no, you are wrong!" Consuelo scrambled to her feet. Meeting his eyes again, she was almost certain that she caught a gleam of something—surely it could not be amusement? She half smiled back. "Is Enrique with you?"

"Can you doubt it?" he said sardonically. "Come now. We are holding up the driver and all these good people."

"Yes, of course." She turned to Mrs. Rudge with quaint courtesy. "I am in safe hands, I promise you. And thank you, señora, for all your great kindness to me. May God go with you."

"Why, bless you, dearie! If that wasn't very prettily said!" cried the old lady, much moved. "It's been a pleasure knowing you . . . you see as you take care, now!"

This last was shouted as Consuelo was lifted and

swung away out of view amid a chorus of good-byes. Henry, at a signal, moved his curricle out of the path of the stage, and the driver whipped up the horses.

"Well now," said Nick, as they stood at the edge of the road with the dust settling around them in the wake of the departing coach. His eyes were crinkled up against the sun so that she could not see his expression, but she supposed that he was awaiting an explanation.

Looked at from his point of view, what she had done was unforgivable, coming as it had on top of all the rest; and now when it was too late, she could see that what she had thought of as a last impulsive bid for freedom simply confirmed her to be what he had dubbed her—"a silly, irresponsible girl."

Ah, well. She straightened her shoulders, gathering the remnants of her pride around her as a shield against his anger. Her determined chin lifted a shade, and as she drew a deep breath and wondered how to begin, the words rushed out unbidden.

"I am so very glad that you came!"

It wasn't at all what she had meant to say. His black brows came together in a most forbidding way, and she braced herself for what must follow.

"Are you?" he said in a strangely unemotional voice. His eyes had opened a little wider and seemed as though they would never look their fill. At last he lifted a finger and ran it lightly down the curve of her throat. "I ought to wring that beautiful little neck," he said softly.

She stood there unmoving, incapable of speech, but with a wild singing in her blood that she had never known before, her head full of incoherent thoughts. It must be the result of so much traveling.

It was Henry, driving up in the curricle and demanding to know if she was all right, who brought her back to reality. She gave herself a quick mental shake and withdrew her gaze from the captain, covering her confusion with a show of spirit.

"Yes, of course I am all right. Whyever should I not be?"

"Because, you idiotish girl, it was a cork-brained idea, rushing off like that!"

Well, really! She had expected to be rebuked by the captain, but she had not looked to be censured by her beloved! "I am not idiotish and it was a splendid idea! Furthermore, I managed very well for myself, I might tell you!"

"Maybe, but suppose we had not been able to come up with you so soon, what then?"

We? Had he then gone over to the enemy? She felt suddenly dispirited. It was futile to quarrel, after all, especially as, remembering the rakish gentleman, she knew that he was right.

"Children," said Nick in exasperation. "Do you think you might reserve your squabbles for a more suitable occasion?"

"I have no wish to squabble with Enrique," said Consuelo in a subdued voice. "It is only that I thought . . ." She shrugged. "Oh, well, it no longer matters what I thought."

"Good." Nick prepared to lift her into the curricle and for a moment his voice hardened. "I don't know if I need to say it, but there will be no more running away."

"Of course not." she sighed. "I can quite see that it is of little use." She would not meet his eyes as he swung her up and climbed in beside her so that they were close-packed together.

"This will be a bit of a squeeze, I'm afraid, but it won't be for very long. Lord Linton will take us back to Welwyn and from there we will take the post chaise which I have already ordered, while he drives back to London ahead of us to dispose of his curricle before joining us at the dock." Nick turned to Henry. "I must ask you to make all speed, my lord. I am determined to leave on the evening tide, and if you aren't there, I shall sail without you."

"I'll be there," said Henry, bridling a little.

Consuelo looked in puzzlement from one to the other as Henry took up the reins.

"I am coming to Spain with you," he explained, glancing down at her with a wry grin. "Beard your father in his den and all that!" And as she strove to respond with enthusiasm to his news: "It seems there ain't any other course left, dearest, and Captain Bannion seams to feel that there is some room for hope, at least."

Consuelo's eyes met the captain's in a brief query.

"I know," he said. "But I believe a case could be made out which your father might reasonably consider."

"Then that is excellent, *querido!*" she told Henry brightly, and wondered why she did not feel any sense of elation.

At Welwyn she was reunited with Floss and was able to return the money the maid had so generously parted with. Nick reassured her that the maid would suffer no blame.

"Since I discovered your absence in almost the same moment that, er, Floss was imparting the news to Lord Linton, I doubt the landlord was ever aware of her part in your escapade."

"Well, I am glad"—Consuelo sighed—"because she was very kind to me."

This brought an unexpected, if ironic, smile. "And the lady in the coach—was she also kind to you?"

"Yes indeed. Also, she shared her hamper of food with me."

"Then you probably fared better than I." Henry sounded faintly aggrieved. "Dashed if I managed more than a couple of mouthfuls before we had to come chasing after you!"

Consuelo was not sorry when they were at last in the post chaise and on their way back to London. It was certainly more comfortable than the curricle, and soon she was leaning back with a sigh, resigned for the moment to whatever fate might decree.

It did seem very strange to be traveling in a closed carriage with only Captain Bannion for company. She had thought she had grown to know him quite well, but now an unaccountable shyness overcame her, and as if he sensed her difficulty, he went out of his way, it seemed, to set her at ease.

Soon they were conversing together most amiably, though occasionally his voice went far away and she was obliged to stifle a yawn. He was in the middle of a most entertaining story about one of his adventures during the war when her head, which had drooped more than once, finally sank against his arm.

Nick, caught in midsentence, looked down at her in wry amusement, which faded as he studied the face now relaxed in sleep, dark lashes fanning out across her cheek and her mouth still curved into a smile from something he had been saying. She had borne up bravely considering that it must be all of thirty-six hours since she had slept.

"Here," he said softly, raising her up so that he could slip his arm behind her to draw her close. She sighed and snuggled her head against his chest, and he felt again the sudden rush of emotion he had experienced upon finding her unharmed in that wretched stagecoach. He had stood there like a fool, staring at her, when all the time he was longing to take her in his arms.

Lord, what a coil! This had been no part of his reckoning. Until now, love had figured but lightly in his life and he had thought to keep it that way.

But somehow this girl, with her curious mixture of child and woman, had touched a chord in him hitherto undreamed of. He knew a fierce desire to protect her, not least from her own foolishness. As for the thought of her marrying a twice-widowed hidalgo as old as her father—the thought disgusted him.

Belatedly Nick reminded himself that Consuelo was in love with Linton, and that he himself had pledged himself to aid their cause. In her mind he probably figured as someone not far short of her father's generation—he had even fostered that image! It was ironical that he should now wish things otherwise.

What, after all, had he to offer a girl of Consuelo's genteel upbringing, even could she be brought to consider him in the light of a suitor? Without his present way of life, he would be a pauper—the heir to a baronetcy riddled with debts, his only claim to property a crumbling mansion on the west coast of Ireland, with every acre of disposable land long since sold off and the remainder mortgaged to the hilt, a prey to rampant neglect. Apply to his mother's family he would not; though they had more than once expressed a willingness to absorb him into their midst, the bonds of his allegiance would soon fetter him in respectability and make him a prisoner of their kindly, but rigid, way of life.

Nick's mouth was set in grim lines as he decided that, feckless though Linton probably was, Consuelo would be better off with him. The only service he could render her would be to persuade her father to allow the match. Yet even as he made the decision, his arm tightened about her. She stirred, but did not wake.

Consuelo was still sound asleep when the post chaise arrived at the London docks. Nick directed the postboys where to go, his heart lifting already at the sights and sounds and smells of the seething port going about its business, the masts and rigging of innumerable ships traced against the sky in the late-afternoon sun.

And here at last was the *Spanish Lady* moving gently at her moorings. Nick managed to lift Consuelo down from the chaise without waking her, and as he carried her up the gangplank he noticed with approval that Bob Fletcher had made good use of the extra time. New paint gleamed everywhere, and the brasswork of the compass, the rims of the portholes, even the boss of the steering wheel had been polished until they shone, the sun glancing off them to send slivers of golden light across the well-scrubbed deck.

Bob's face shone, too, with all the effort, his skin tanned to that curious shade of ruddy bronze that went with sandy hair. Yet Nick sensed an uneasiness about him. His pleasant features wore a troubled frown as he beheld Nick's burden.

Nick at once jumped to conclusions. "Don't tell me that those confounded women haven't arrived?"

"Oh, they've arrived, right enough. Leastways . . ."

Before he could complete the sentence there was a faint clattering of feet on the companionway and a head emerged, an outrageously stylish bonnet tied becomingly under one ear.

"Good God!" said Nick blankly.

Verena Covington stepped gracefully up on the

deck, her green eyes resting thoughtfully on Consuelo's sleeping form cradled so intimately in his arms.

"Good evening, Nicholas," she said with a lift of her delicate brows. "We were beginning to wonder if you would come in time."

Chapter 10

Consuelo stirred, and for a moment wondered where she was. Then she remembered. The post chaise . . . she must have fallen alseep! How impolite Captain Bannion would think her! And then, as full consciousness returned she became aware that she was being carried in someone's arms; there was fresh air on her cheeks, and though it did not seem possible, she thought she heard Lady Covington's voice.

Out of sheer curiosity she opened her eyes—and found Captain Bannion's face close above her. He looked very stern, but as she uttered a little exclamation he looked down at her, and for a moment his expression softened.

"Well," he said. "When you sleep, you sleep!"

She felt the color creeping into her face. "I am sorry. Please, you may put me down now!"

He did so, but kept a steadying arm about her. Consuelo turned her head and realized that they were on board ship, and in the same moment she saw Lady Covington.

"Oh, it *was* you! I thought I had dreamed your voice. But I don't understand . . ."

"It is really quite simple, my dear. Your duenna is unfit for the journey and I am to stand in her place."

"Oh, but . . . there is surely no need . . ." Consuelo stammered.

"Lady Covington's laugh tinkled. "My dear child . . . as if I could think of your returning to your papa so ill chaperoned!"

Consuelo's glance flew instinctively to the captain, who in turn was looking at Lady Covington with a most curious expression in his eyes. She remembered what Enrique had said about them . . . was it then true that they were in love? It seemed entirely possible. Perhaps this little scheme to take the place of Señora Diaz (which she could not think at all necessary) had been arranged by them. The idea confused her, and she did not know what to say.

But she was spared the necessity, for Captain Bannion was calling forward a man with sand-colored hair and a shy smile, introducing him and bidding him escort her below where Maria awaited her.

"Then get back here pretty sharpish, if you please, Mr. Fletcher. The wind is veering and enough time has been wasted already."

"But . . . Enrique?" cried Consuelo.

"I am sorry, señorita." Nick was curt with her. "But Lord Linton knew my intentions. If he is not here within the next ten minutes we must sail without him."

She turned away to follow Mr. Fletcher, knowing from his tone that to argue was pointless. Behind her Lady Convington was saying in her amused way: "Lud! Never tell me that Henry is minded to come to Spain, also?" She did not hear the captain's reply.

Below, in a tiny cramped cabin that had been skillfully adapted to accommodate three females, Consuelo was reunited with Maria. Mr. Fletcher, having seen her safely bestowed, apologized for the lack of those comforts he accounted necessary for a lady's well-being and begged to be excused, leaving her to endure Maria's many exclamations of joy and relief. The much-tried maid's tears flowed afresh as she caught sight of Consuelo's raggedly shorn hair, now settled into a thick tousled bob about her ears. Normally such behavior would bring a sharp rebuke, but now her young mistress scarcely seemed to notice, as she submitted without protest to having her crumpled gown changed for a fresh one. Moreover, she showed little inclination to confide her adventures, no matter how skillfully she was coaxed.

A deep depression seemed to have settled upon her spirits—not to be wondered at, perhaps, what with her disappointment and nothing but trouble facing her, or so Maria reckoned, let anyone tell her different.

And then, almost as the ship began to move, there came a great to-ing and fro-ing above and a clattering on the companionway. There was a sharp rap on the door and it opened to admit Lord Linton.

"Lord!" he exclaimed as Consuelo spun around. "That was a close-run thing! They were just hauling in the gangplank!"

Later she stood at the taffrail with him as the schooner moved slowly downriver toward the widening estuary and the open sea beyond. She was hardly aware of all the activity going on around her. Her eyes were fixed resolutely on the receding spires and chimneys of London, which seemed to be afire in the evening sun. Her heart was heavy with the fatalistic certainty that she would never see it again, a mood that all of Enrique's determined joviality could not touch.

"Cheer up, Consuelo," he urged. "Only consider, when we return, it will be as man and wife."

She could not share his certainty and so did not

reply. The brim of her bonnet hid her face so that he could not read her expression, but it did occur to him that she had been behaving very oddly ever since he had come aboard. He was prey to a sudden unease.

"That *is* what you want, is it not?" he demanded urgently. "I mean . . . you haven't changed your mind?"

"Oh, I am sorry, Enrique!" Consuelo made a determined effort to pull herself together. She turned to him, stretching out her hand impulsively. "I am behaving very badly, I know. But today has been so strange. Do you not find it so? I feel . . . oh, I do not know exactly how I feel, but it is not the least like myself."

"Well, it ain't every day you set out to elope!" He half grinned. "Lord, it seems like a lifetime since we left Covington Manor." He lowered his voice. "And what do you think of Verena turning up like that? Very prettily arranged, I must say?"

"You think it was arranged?" Consuelo asked casually. "I thought that the captain seemed taken aback."

"Well, he would, wouldn't he? I mean, the lady's honor and all that! But Verena ain't one to put herself about without some encouragement. She must be infatuated to have exerted herself thus far!"

Consuelo wished she had not asked. It did not seem quite proper to be discussing Lady Covington and Captain Bannion in so free a fashion.

Supper that evening was not the easiest of meals. The captain was wholly occupied on deck, and in his absence Consuelo could not but notice her ladyship's moodiness. She picked at her food and complained constantly of its lack of savor, and when Enrique had the temerity to tease her, she snapped at him.

After supper, they remained in the surprisingly spacious saloon. It was low-pitched and was paneled in oak with long cushioned seats along the bulkhead and beneath the porthole. The table and chairs were also of oak, as was a handsome sideboard topped by a case of cut-glass flagons. And a glass-fronted bookcase crammed with books betrayed its owner's tastes.

Lady Covington declined to play cards, but sat watching the young couple's good-natured squabbles over a game of brag in a brooding silence and finally excused herself, pleading a slight headache.

"Frustration, more like!" Henry grinned knowingly as the door closed, but Consuelo declined to comment.

The two young people played on for a while, with Consuelo struggling to stifle her yawns. Finally she sat back.

"I believe, Enrique, that I, too, must go to my bed before I begin to fall asleep."

Henry saw that her face was smudged with weariness. He held out a hand. "Come and take a turn on deck first? Decidedly beneficial, you know—a little exercise before retiring."

Consuelo hesitated—and then sighed. "Very well, *querido*."

It was very strange on deck, as though they were in a vast shadowy void through which the schooner cleaved its way with instinctive sureness. A slight mist obscured the sky, but a faint luminosity cast an occasional pewterlike glimmer over the gently swelling waves.

Henry watched the pensive profile of the girl at his side for a moment and then traced a finger along the delicate outline of her jaw.

"Do you love me, little Consuelo?" he asked softly. She started a little at his touch, seeming to come back from a great distance. She turned to look up at him and her eye was caught by two shadows moving against the stern rail. Moonlight caught the glint of fair hair, a light breeze carried the murmur of voices, a husky laugh . . . the two figures moved close, merging into one. . . .

"Yes, of course I do!" she declared with so much fervor that he was taken aback.

And it was true, she assured herself later as she lay waiting for sleep. Had she not loved Enrique from the very first? Had she not seen in him everything that she might conceivably wish for. Perhaps he was a little too amiable, too easily led on occasion, but that surely could not be accounted a fault?

From beneath veiled lashes she watched Lady Covington come into the cabin. The lamp, swaying gently on its gimbal, revealed a faint aura of triumph about her as she made ready to retire, sending poor Maria scurrying to do her bidding.

Consuela wondered briefly why such a revelation should fill her with so much dissatisfaction. And then she slept.

She slept heavily, lulled by the ship's motion, and awoke early, roused by some sound—a strange monotonous rasping, accompanied by a low moaning noise. She opened her eyes to see the lamp swinging in an ominous arc above her and, lifting on one elbow, found the poor light sufficient to show her Lady Covington lying prostrate, one hand pressed across her eyes as her head moved restlessly back and forth.

Consuelo swung her legs over the side of the cotlike bed and stood upright, staggering as the floor moved beneath her. "Are you feeling unwell, señora?" she asked anxiously, leaning over the older woman. "Is there anything I can do for you?"

The hand lifted momentarily to reveal anguished eyes, which stared resentfully up into the fresh young face. Consuelo was shocked to see the change in her beautiful companion, and as if the thought communicated itself, the hand came down abruptly, and Lady Covington turned to the wall.

"Go away!" she muttered peevishly. "That girl of yours is tending to me."

Consuelo shrugged, and since there was no sign of Maria she began to clamber into her clothes unaided —an exercise requiring a certain expertise. She had almost finished when there was a fumbling at the door which opened to admit Maria, clasping a large jug in her arms. The maid looked almost as gray-faced as Lady Covington.

"Oh, poor Maria!" she exclaimed. "You should be lying down also."

"Do not be concerned for me, señorita," came the stoical reply. "My condition is not desperate."

"Even so . . ."

"Is that Maria with the water?" Lady Covington's voice was sharp. "I cannot imagine what has taken you so long . . . consorting with some vulgar little sailor, no doubt, while I lie here burning up with thirst and fever! You are all alike!"

"You shall not speak to Maria in that way!" cried Consuelo, incensed.

Maria shook her head. "It is unimportant."

"But you are not obliged to wait upon Lady Covington. It is not your place!"

"That is as may be, but how do I tell *her* that?" said the maid dryly. And then, a trifle impatiently: "I do not mind, señorita—truly!"

"Ah, dear God, how my head throbs!" The voice was plaintive once more. "Maria, you must bathe it with rosewater—in the small casket beside my portmanteau."

"You had best go," Maria advised, putting down the jug and giving her mistress an encouraging push toward the door—and because Consuelo felt herself unwanted by either of them, she went.

The main cabin was empty, though there were signs that someone had breakfasted there not too long since. There came a quick step and she turned, hoping to see Enrique, but it was only Mr. Fletcher. He blushed, said good morning and hoped that she had slept well.

"Thank you—yes. But Lady Covington did not. I fear she is most unwell." Consuelo sighed. "Is En—Is Lord Linton about yet, do you know?"

"No, nor likely to be in the near future." He nodded sympathetically, seeing her look of dismay. "I'm afraid so—sick as a dog!"

"Oh, no!" she wailed. "Not Enrique, also! How . . . how very poor-spirited of him . . ." She stopped suddenly, a hand to her mouth, as she realized how unfeeling that must sound. "Of course I am very sorry for him. Is he very ill? Can I go to him?"

"Yes he is—and no, I don't advise it," said Mr. Fletcher with a twinkle. "If I were you, I should have some breakfast, always supposing that you feel like eating."

The cabin heaved as though lifted by a giant hand, sending the crockery skittering across the table before coming to rest against its protective rail, to which Consuelo clung until she was flung unceremoniously on to the settee.

"Madre de Dios!"

"The ship is heeling with the wind," Bob Fletcher told her apologetically, "and we've a pretty strong sea running. Are you all right, señorita?"

"I believe so." She laughed and hastily rearranged her skirts.

There was a clatter of feet on the companionway and Captain Bannion came in, pulling off a short thick coat.

"Ah, there you are, Mr. Fletcher," he said, eyeing the laughing couple dourly. "That sea is the very devil. The waves so crosshatched, I'll swear they're hell-bent on private insurrection! We'll have the top-sail reefed, if you please. Good morning, señorita." As his first officer departed with a cheery smile Nick turned his attention to her, as though he had but that moment seen her. "All alone?"

She explained about Enrique, and about Lady Covington and Maria.

"I am sorry," he said. "Seasickness can be the very devil, and there is little can be done for it. I have a cordial which will ease their thirst, if nothing else." He frowned. "Perhaps I will step along later to discover if there is anything I can do to help make her ladyship more comfortable."

Some imp of mischief was urging Consuelo to encourage him; how disillusioned he would be to find Lady Covington looking so haggard! She blushed for such base thoughts and said quickly: "I should not, if I were you. I believe she would not care to have you see her looking less than her best!"

Nick regarded her somewhat quizzically. "That is a very perceptive remark for one so young."

"Not at all." She sat up very straight. "I am a woman also, and know how it must be, though I doubt I should care so very much in a like situation."

He seemed amused.

Consuelo's shoulders dropped a fraction. "Mr. Fletcher says I must not visit Enrique for the same reason!" She sighed heavily.

"Poor little Consuelo! So you are the sole survivor." The boat pitched and rolled back with a slow pendulum swing. He kept his balance with an ease she could not but admire, and sketched her a bow. "Then will you do your captain the honor of taking breakfast with him, señorita? Or are you also feeling queasy?"

Her mouth curved upward enchantingly. "I should be pleased to do so, señor. Perhaps it betrays in me a disgraceful lack of sensibility, but to own the truth, I am excessively hungry!"

Nick laughed aloud. "Good girl! We'll make a sailor of you yet!" He called for his steward, gave orders and then came back to sit opposite her, watching her as the steward cleared away the used dishes. "I fear I cannot vouch for the quality of the food. This kind of weather sets all the pots and pans crashing in the galley and makes our cook confoundedly bad-tempered!"

"We are a great trouble to you, I think," she said shyly as she struggled her way through thick unladylike slices of bread and appalling coffee, black and bitter, which she laced heavily with sugar.

Nick denied the suggestion with suitable gallantry.

"But we are occupying your cabin, are we not—Lady Covington and I?" she insisted. "There was a book of yours on the chest of drawers."

"That isn't any problem. I can sleep anywhere."

A tiny frown puckered her brow. "But . . . Enrique is sharing Mr. Fletcher's cabin, so where *are* you sleeping?"

He lifted an eyebrow, which suggested that the question might be considered impertinent, and she blushed.

"Perhaps I should not have asked."

"My dear child, there is no mystery." He indicated with his head. "I have a hammock slung in the chart room."

Consuelo stated. "That is surely impossible? It is little more than a cubbyhole!"

"You don't need a drawing room to sling a hammock," he said dryly and stood up, thus effectively putting an end to the conversation. "And now, señorita, I must leave you. I fear you are in for a rather wearisome time on your own, but you are welcome to make use of my books, or . . ."

"Can I come up on deck?"

Nick frowned. "I think not. With conditions as they are, it's no place for a lady."

"Oh, please!" she coaxed. "I should not mind the rough weather, and I promise not to be in anyone's way."

Nick looked into the eager shining face and lifted his shoulders in acquiescence. "You won't enjoy it much," he warned.

But Consuelo soon proved him wrong. She enjoyed the whole experience enormously. Wrapped in her cloak, which was soon soaked by the pillars of spray that rose and scoured the deck incessantly, she clung to the rail and listened to the wind screaming defiance at the clear blue sky, shrieking through the rigging and dying every now and then to a sibilant muttering. She watched the crew staggering like drunken men as the schooner pitched and wallowed in the fractious waves. And when Mr. Fletcher came to ask if she was all right, she could only laugh and nod, the words drowned in wind and spray.

Later in the morning she went below to see how the invalids fared. She found Maria utterly exhausted, scarcely able any longer to keep going.

"This is absurd," she said imperiously, chivvying the maid across to her own bed. "You will lie down here and try to sleep. No, I insist! You cannot possibly be comfortable on that makeshift bed on the floor. See, you are to drink some of this good cordial which Captain Bannion has provided . . . there is plenty for both you and Lady Covington."

She took some cordial across to Verena who had watched the affecting scene with acute displeasure. "You will ruin that idle girl," she told Consuelo as the latter raised her up so that she might drink. "They are all alike, believe me. If one does not deal firmly with them from the first . . ."

"Maria is not idle, but very sick—more so than you, I think!" Consuelo would not have believed she could speak so coldly to Lady Covington, who was shaken momentarily out of her self-pity to stare. "Is there anything that I may get for you?"

Verena Covington moved restively. "I want nothing but solid ground beneath my feet—if I do not die in the meantime!" she added, a shade theatrically, and in a lower voice: "I must have been mad to come!"

Consuelo was tempted to agree with her, and to say that she was well served for attempting to use the situation for her own ends, but the impertinence of such a remark too strongly contradicted her upbringing to find utterance, and a glance at the ravaged face brought sudden sympathy.

"You will feel differently," she said more kindly, "when the rough weather abates and you are able to take some fresh air."

Her charity went for the most part unheeded, however, Verena being much too obsessed with her condition to recognize such commiseration as being prompted by anything other than a total lack of sensibility. "You are fortunate to remain unafflicted by the frailty which strikes down the rest of us," she snapped.

"Oh, I am having a splendid time! Captain Bannion is looking after me very well." Consuelo turned to the door without seeing the frigid look on Lady Covington's face.

She was heartily glad to leave the rank, stifling atmosphere of the cabin behind her, and it was with a growing sense of freedom that she scrambled up the companionway once more.

Mr. Fletcher saluted her from the tiny poop as, buffeted by the wind, she made her way crablike along the deck to where Captain Bannion stood braced against a stanchion, squinting into some kind of instrument.

He heard rather than saw her, and said without pausing from what he was doing, "So you haven't yet tired of being at the mercy of the elements?"

"Certainly not."

"How is Lady Covington?"

"Better, I believe, though she does not think it herself."

She thought he chuckled, though it was difficult to be sure with most of his face obscured.

"Very perspicacious! Let us hope that she is permitted to sustain her recovery." He gestured with his head to where a bank of clouds sulfurous and menacing, stretched across the horizon before them.

"A storm?" Consuelo felt a faint flutter of apprehension. A storm on land was one thing, but at sea . . . ?

"We'll be lucky to miss it," he mused, not giving her his whole attention. She studied the instrument with some curiosity.

"What are you doing?" she asked, emboldened by his amiability at breakfast this morning and since.

"Preparing to measure the altitude of the sun." He glanced down at her, grinning at her air of puzzlement.

"A nautical day runs from noon to noon," he explained. "And noon is determined with the aid of this sextant by the moment when the sun reaches its zenith. See . . ." He glanced calculatingly at the sun, then looked into the eyepiece of the instrument, quickly adjusted a clamp on the arm and put it into Consuelo's hands. "Now . . . find the horizon and the sun, and bring them together."

She took the sextant eagerly, squinting down the eyepiece with bated breath. At first she could see nothing and then the horizon came into view, but it was dipping and wavering all over the place.

"Oh, no!" she cried, staggering as the ship lurched. "It won't stay still . . . and I cannot find the sun at all."

He laughed and pulled her in front of him, made a quick adjustment once more and wrapped his arms tightly about her to hold her steady. "Take your time," he said. "Now do you see the sun?"

Its image whirled and danced into view in the tiny mirror, and she squeaked with excitement.

"Carefully now; wait until it just touches the horizon and then tighten the clamp."

She concentrated fiercely, and then with an exultant cry she screwed the clamp tight and held the sextant up to him. He read off the altitude and chuckled softly.

"Have I not done it correctly?" she wailed, lifting to him a face glowing and vividly alive.

"Not quite. But you can't expect to be proficient *so* soon." Still smiling, he glanced quickly at the sun and Consuelo watched the strong angles of his face as he put the sextant to his eye, completely engrossed in what he was doing. She was suddenly very much aware of his close proximity and wondered if she

should move, but remained where she was—a little
breathless, for fear of disturbing him.

He seemed to be taking an unconscionable time,
moving the arm along the scale, waiting—then all at
once, he screwed the clamp firmly and called: time!"

Mr. Fletcher, waiting on the poop above them,
with his timepiece in his hand, reset it and struck the
ship's bell eight times. There came an instant scuffling as the men on watch changed over.

"Do you do this every day?" she asked, entranced
by the romantic concept of it all.

"Every day," he said, resetting his own watch and
looking down at her as though he was surprised to
find her there.

"You are a little like God, I think." She giggled.
"You say it is noon—and behold, it is noon!"

"Oh, we haven't finished yet." He offered a hand
invitingly, and without hesitation she put hers into
it, her fingers curling confidently around his.

Together they went below to the chart room where
he wound and set the ship's chronometer and a second one tucked away in a special compartment, resting on carefully balanced gimbals. This, he told her,
showed the time at Greenwich and never varied
more than a fraction of a second in a day. The two
were compared; she watched as he noted the difference, set down the sextant's reading and proceeded
to plot their course.

He explained it all to her as he went along, but at
the end she shook her head in helpless confusion.

"It is much too difficult, but quite enthralling—
and I am very pleased that you showed me, for I
have never enjoyed anything half so well!"

He stood up. "I am remiss. It's high time you got
out of that wet cloak before you take a chill. I'll see if
cook can be persuaded to produce some drinkable

coffee"—his eyebrow lifted quizzically—"perhaps we should even dose you with a wee tot . . ."

"Tot?"

"Rum," he explained, grinning. "Just to be sure."

"Ugh!" Consuelo pulled a face. "No, I thank you!"

She didn't want the moment to end but could think of nothing to detain him. As they passed through the doorway leading from the chart room to the main cabin the ship heaved, throwing her hard against his chest. His arms closed around her for protection and remained there, as, with laughter subsiding, their eyes met—and held. His were very brilliant, very blue, and there was something in their depths that induced in her a sweet suffocating sensation; there was a weakness in her limbs so that she would have fallen had he not been holding her so tightly.

"Consuelo?" he murmured softly, half wonderingly.

"Señor?"

His head was bent very close. He was about to kiss her, she knew, and in a corner of her mind she wondered why she had never felt remotely like this when Enrique had kissed her. Her heart was fluttering right up in her throat now, and she was beginning to tremble. She closed her eyes . . .

Chapter 11

"Consuelo?"

It was a different voice, sharp, familiar—coming from a long way off. She wanted it to go away again so that she might explore to the full all these wonderful sensations that were coursing through her.

But Captain Bannion was already releasing her, setting her firmly on her feet and striding away to assist Lady Covington, who stood swaying just within the doorway of the main cabin. Valiantly she took a step and clung to the sideboard for support, looking incredibly lovely, incredibly frail in a white floating peignoir, her fair hair cascading around a face filled with pale vulnerable shadows, its only color the pouting mouth beguilingly touched with pink.

He reached her side and she leaned heavily upon him as he guided her toward the settee. "I feel so stupidly weak"—she sighed in answer to his terse inquiry, her voice no more than a thread of that initial sharp utterance—"but I felt I could no longer neglect my responsibility for dear Consuelo. I do hope the child has not usurped too much of your valuable time?"

Nick did not reply, could not reply, he was so full of impotent rage. Granite-faced, he made her comfortable, fetching a blanket when she prettily complained of feeling a draft and tucking it about her with hands that shook slightly from a suppressed urge to wrap themselves around her elegant neck. Then he pleaded a necessity to return to his duties.

"Of course." she smiled sweetly. "We would not dream of keeping you from them!"

Consuelo was still standing where he had left her. There was a curious blankness in her eyes, and he saw that she was trembling visibly now. He silently cursed himself for frightening her and was obliged to fight down an overwhelming urge to snatch her up in his arms and carry her forever out of reach of her father, of Don Miguel—and most of all, of Henry Linton. But, he reminded himself, Consuelo was in love with her "Enrique". . . .

So he avoided her eyes and said harshly as he left, "For heaven's sake, do go and get out of that sodden cloak, or we shall have another invalid on our hands!"

She went on standing there for several minutes after he had gone, attempting to take herself in hand. A torrent of conflicting emotions bewildered and threatened to engulf her. More than anything, she was hurt by Captain Bannion's sudden change of manner toward her. Hampered by a painful lack of experience, she could find but one explanation: she had misunderstood him, and was immediately terrified lest she had given herself away. How foolish he would think her should he ever guess with what wild inaccuracy she had interpreted those few brief moments of intimacy.

Yet surely she could not have been *so* mistaken? She recalled his silence when Lady Covington had implied that she had been a nuisance, the swiftness with which he had hurried to Lady Covington's side—

and jealousy, an emotion until now quite foreign to her nature, washed over her in waves.

Verena Covington watched her with narrowed eyes. The chit was displaying all the symptoms of emotional shock. So she had not imagined Consuelo's growing interest in Nick Bannion and his in her. Her own ardor was fast withering, its roots too shallow to withstand the exigencies of this intolerable voyage. But with egoistical petty-mindedness she declined to relinquish the role she had designated for herself to a mere untried slip of a girl.

"Gracious!" she exclaimed with a faint derisive laugh. "What a little urchin you *do* look, my dear! One really wonders what Captain Bannion must have thought of you!"

Consuelo winced, but from somewhere within pride came to her rescue. "I am sure you are right," she said quietly. "Forgive me, I must go to tidy myself and put my cloak to dry."

It was pride that made her return presently to sit with Lady Covington, determined to behave as though nothing had happened. There was a jug of coffee on the table, cups set on damp mats to stop them from sliding about and some rather solid-looking biscuits.

"Can I pour you some?" she asked in a deliberately bright voice.

Verena pulled a face. "I think not. I was asking the steward about Henry," she said casually. "It appears he may be contemplating joining us before long. You will like that, won't you?"

Consuelo's reply was indistinct, half submerged in her cup. She was glad of the coffee's bitterness, which was only marginally less than it had been at breakfast—its very acridity took her mind off even more bitter thoughts.

After a while, little attempt was made on either

side to talk. Lady Covington, though much recovered, seemed disinclined to exert herself and fell to dozing, and Consuelo, left to her own unhappy thoughts, soon found her own eyelids beginning to flutter.

She was woken from an oppressive dream, in which Captain Bannion was giving her away in marriage with inexorable formality to Don Miguel, by a violent explosion of sound, which seemed to set the schooner shuddering down to its very bowels.

In the nearby sleeping cabin, Maria shrieked in terror and Consuelo was jerked to her feet, heart pounding, to find herself in near darkness, which in that same instant exploded into eye-searing brilliance to show Lady Covington cowering in her corner, her whimpered "Oh, God! Oh, God!" immediately cut off by a clap of thunder overhead that seemed to be tearing the heavens asunder.

Without even pausing to fetch her cloak, she rushed up on deck—and there halted. *"Madre de Dios!"* she breathed, instinctively crossing herself.

It was like the end of the world.

The sky ahead glowed like a giant caldron, spewing out streams of molten metal that rolled and trickled toward the fiery rim of the horizon, while behind and all about them the towering clouds were being rent into black tattered rags by the lightning, which pulsed and flickered and forked incessantly to the accompanying tumult of crashing thunder.

Consuelo clung to the rail, staring in awe at the heaving, leaden sea where a wave of frightening size seemed to be bearing down on them. She heard Captain Bannion yelling to the crew to "wear ship! All hands wear ship!" as he struggled to master the wheel.

He turned and caught sight of her, and she saw the dawning of horror in his face as he gestured frantically for her to get below. But she was wholly spell-bound by the sight before her, and her limbs would not obey her.

And then it was too late.

The water was upon her in a roaring, drowning cascade that flattened her eyelids against her eyes and made breathing an impossibility. She gasped and swallowed a vile, choking quantity of water . . . and in the same moment her hands were wrenched from the rail and she was swept off her feet and flung like a sodden rag doll with bone-jarring force against the wheel housing.

She came to her senses to hear her name being shouted hoarsely above the roar of the storm. Hands were feeling her limbs, lifting her; she groaned and retched violently from the effects of the swallowed seawater, and finally opened her eyes to find rainlike rods of fiery light in the flash and flare beating down upon her.

Seen through stinging eyes, Captain Bannion's face was a wet blur, his voice a mingled confusion of anger and anguish as he demanded to know if she was hurt.

"Little fool!" His tongue roughly chastised her over and over. "You crazy little fool, you might easily have been killed!"

His upbraiding had a strangely beneficial effect upon her. "But I am not, as you can see," she gasped, struggling to stand with some semblance of dignity and relieved to see that all around her men were clambering to their feet, having been similarly felled by the torrent. "My head aches a little and I shall have bruises tomorrow, but that is all."

"All!" He ground the words out, scooping her up into his arms despite her protests. "You are confound-edly complacent, I must say!"

At the head of the companionway she insisted that he put her down." I can manage very well, I promise you. You really must not concern yourself with me when there are so many important matters needing your attention."

He seemed set to argue, but Mr. Fletcher's voice calling him was too urgent to be ignored. As he set her down she met his still-lowering glance with what she hoped was a confident smile and made her way slowly and painfully below, where she was met with a shriek of dismay from Lady Covington. Verena reacted as though Consuelo had been some monster dredged up by the storm. Then Henry Linton, who had stumbled, white and shaking, from his cabin at the height of the storm, rose unsteadily from the place where he had collapsed upon learning of Consuelo's extraordinary behavior and grimaced fastidiously upon finding his feet in a pool of water.

"God in heaven, Consuelo! You look . . . you look . . . dammit, I'm not sure I wish to confess how you look! Have you run mad? Whatever can have possessed you to venture on deck at such a time?"

It did not seem to occur to either of them to inquire after her well-being. A lump came in her throat. One might be forgiven for expecting some measure of concern if she looked as dreadful as they inplied. But then, she concluded grudgingly, they had both been under a measure of strain themselves.

She stood with her sodden dress slowly adding to the wetness of the floor and lifted her hands in a gesture of resignation. "I . . . had better go now to change out of these clothes."

Maria's welcome more than made up for any previous lack. She fell upon her mistress as upon one come back from the dead, crying and laughing at the same time, throwing up her hands in horror at the sight of the great weals and bruises already disfiguring the fair skin as she stripped off Consuelo's wet clothes.

Maria had, it seemed, run screaming into the main cabin at the height of the storm. "I was so frightened, señorita! And when Lady Covington told me, sobbing, that you had gone out into the storm, I was sure that you would never be heard of again. I crept back here and buried my head under the blankets and wished to die!"

Consuelo, with her head throbbing and every bit of her aching, let Maria babble on without really listening. Her eyes still felt sore from the seawater as she regarded the bed longingly. If the cabin hadn't still had the stench of sickness about it, she would have succumbed there and then. Perhaps, if the storm wears itself out, something may be done to freshen it . . . the effort of coherent thought made her head ache the more.

The light was much improved when she returned wearily to sit with the others. The cabin showed much evidence of its recent upheaval, but the schooner was already moving more easily, and it appeared that the tempest, having wreaked its will upon them, had now passed over, though any inclination to discover this at first hand had left her.

There seemed to be little inclination for conversation. Consuelo roused herself to ask Enrique whether he was feeling better, and, upon receiving a somewhat grudging admission that he was, told him—with less than perfect truth—how much she had missed him. Verena, in a sudden burst of spleen, observed that never had she traveled so miserably or with so little regard for her comfort, and that the sooner she could get back home, the better pleased she would be . . . which prompted Henry to say, with unusual force, that she was here entirely by her own choice, and if the outcome was not to her liking, she could hardly set the blame at anyone else's door. After which, communication lapsed.

When Mr. Fletcher presently came in carrying a young boy, the three were sitting in a constrained silence.

The lad was no more than thirteen or fourteen and small for his age. He looked very white beneath his weather-tanned skin as Mr. Fletcher lowered him carefully to the part of the settee swiftly vacated by Consuelo.

"I wonder"—Mr. Fletcher addressed them all apologetically—"if you would mind keeping an eye on young Batty here until the captain can get down to take a look at him?"

"Well, really! Doesn't he rather belong in his own quarters?" Verena asked pointedly.

"Yes, ma'am, and in the ordinary way, that's where he would be, but it's clear the lad has a broken arm, and it will be for the captain to set it as best he can. Not much room for that sort of thing in crew's quarters, ma'am." Bob Fletcher was much too well-mannered to issue a direct reproof to a lady, but the implication lay unspoken in the soft burr of his voice.

"Is the storm quite over now, Mr. Fletcher?" Consuelo asked, moving impulsively to the boy's side, her own hurts for the moment forgotten.

"It is, señorita. But there's a fair deal of clearing up to be done; one of the jib's was carried clean away, and the rest . . . well . . ." He gave her a searching look, paused and said diffidently, "That was a nasty experience you had just now, señorita. Shouldn't you be lying down?"

"Later," she said, her hand reaching out to the boy's good one. "I am all right."

He smiled and nodded. Before he left them he went into the chart room and returned with a small keg from which he poured a generous measure. "Rum," he said in a low voice, looking particularly at Lord Linton. "Get as much down him as you can. He's going to need it."

His lordship nodded, but looked apprehensive. "Here now, young shaver," he said with false heartiness, bringing the cup across. "This'll put new life into you, I shouldn't wonder!"

Consuelo put her other arm under the boy's head to lift it so that he might drink, and found his eyes fixed unwaveringly on her. She smiled sympathetically, alarmed to see how the bone protruded. "Is your poor arm very painful, Batty?"

He bit his lip. "S'aw right, miss," he said valiantly.

"Batty? That is a jolly sort of name."

"It's Bartholomew really, miss. Bartholomew Twig, but I've allus been called Batty."

He was shivering, and Consuelo ran to get a blanket from her bed. She returned to find Enrique giving him more rum. She swiftly tucked the blanket around him and settled back beside him once more, stifling a groan as she was made aware of her bruises.

"Consuelo!" Verena expostulated. "There is no need to make such a fuss over the boy. You have only just changed your dress, and now look at you, kneeling there on the damp, and doubtless dirty, floor. And Henry is little better! This whole ridiculous affair is getting out of hand!"

"But you cannot begrudge Batty a little comfort when he is in dreadful pain?"

"It en't quite so bad now, miss." Batty's words were beginning to slur a little.

Henry straightened up with a faintly malicious smile. "You see, my dear, Consuelo is blessed with a soft heart," he said and had the satisfaction of seeing Verena's lips tightened. He sighed with resignation. "I had hoped that a little of it might be expended on me!"

"Ah, *querido,* I am indeed sorry that you have been so unwell!" Consuelo threw him a swift consoling smile. "But you must see that a broken limb is so much worse than mere *mal de mer,* and Batty is very young."

"Why've you got hair cut like a boy?" drawled the object of her sympathy, made bold by his tipsy condition.

She grinned and reached up a hand to a much-disheveled Enrique as she leaned forward to confide with a giggle, "Because I was eloping with this fine gentleman who is Lord Linton!" She was rewarded with a sleepy chuckle.

"Elopin'." He yawned hugely. "That's rich, that is!"

It was into this scene of apparent merriment that Nick walked, having steeled himself to perform one of his less pleasant duties. After an hour that had seemed like a year when they had come closer to disaster than he cared to remember, he was bone-weary, sick at heart and in no humor to appreciate the spectacle of Consuelo on her knees, enjoying the company of Linton and young Batty, while he had been doing his best to put from his mind the thought of her lying prostrate after her ordeal.

It made him short to the point of curtness when, having taken in the scene and looked to Verena Covington, she had merely shrugged her beautiful shoulders and dismissed it with: "I know, but don't look to me, Nicholas—my word counts for less than nothing!"

Consuelo scrambled to her feet, an exercise not

easily accomplished without some discomfort, as he was quick to note. She disarmed him almost at once, however, by her obvious concern for Batty, apparent in her explanation and the way the boy still clung to her hand.

"Well, you appear to have done your best to render him insensible," he said dryly. "It should make my task that much simpler."

He motioned to a large, rather rough-looking man who had followed him in and stood just inside the door, shuffling his feet.

"We'll have him on the table, Joe; and see if you can do anything with that lamp. The daylight will be gone soon and I want as much light as I can get." Nick turned to the others. "I have no wish to appear inhospitable, but I feel you will be happier elsewhere whilst I am endeavouring to make young Batty more comfortable."

Verena rose and drifted with appealing frailty toward the door. "I couldn't agree with you more. My nerves have already sustained more than they are accustomed to these past few hours. I certainly have no desire to witness your unpleasant ministrations, however skilled a bone setter you may be! Come Consuelo."

But Consuelo's hand was still being gripped painfully by Batty, and befuddled senses had somewhat absorbed the gist of what was about to happen.

"Don' go!" he pleaded, terror mingled with the confusion in his eyes, clinging on even as the big man lifted him.

The slurred plea went straight to Consuelo's heart. "Of course I am not going anywhere, *amigo*."

"Oh yes you are," said Nick harshly, as Henry, too, began to remonstrate with her.

"And it will not be so bad, you will see," she

continued doggedly, ignoring their interruptions, "because Captain Bannion is a very clever man and knows exactly what to do for your poor arm!"

"Consuelo," Nick warned. "I am in no mood . . ."

"Consuelo," Henry coaxed. "Come with me. You should go and rest for a little while . . . and I mean to wash and change, so that I shall feel very much more the thing. And we can meet again later, when all this is over."

"I can't get this lamp to hang no lower, Cap'n," grunted Joe in growing exasperation.

"Then it is simple," said Consuelo. "I will hold the lamp for you, and you can then have it as close as you please." She met the captain's narrowed eyes with such solemn entreaty and sheer determination that their fierceness gradually faded to wry resignation.

"What a very persistent girl you are," he said in the oddest voice. "I wonder that I should even trouble to argue! Very well, then; you may stay, *and* hold the lamp if you insist, but no talk, no distractions of any kind—and for God's sake, don't you dare to faint on me!"

"As if I would!" She was indignant.

"Well, I think that accident you had during the storm must have addled your wits!" said Henry in blunt disapproval. "But I doubt my opinion counts for very much. I shall hope to see you later, if you haven't knocked yourself up entirely in the meantime!" He left rather hurriedly, before he, too, could be pressed into service.

"For once I find myself in agreement with Lord Linton," said Nick, busily assembling all that he would need for his unwelcome task. "But we've already kept Batty waiting long enough." He looked down at the slight figure stretched out on the table and there was nothing in his quiet confident smile to betray the terrible uncertainty within him. "You ready, boy?"

Batty's glazed eyes widened a little and his fingers bit deeper into Consuelo's hand as Joe's massive paws came down to hold him rigid. But almost as soon as Nick began to explore the extent of his injury he lost consciousness.

"Well, that's a mercy," Nick said.

"Looks a rare old mess, Cap'n," Joe observed dourly. "Reckon as you'll do well to save that un."

Consuelo felt her heart turn over. Her glance flew to Nick's face. "Oh, but surely . . ." The lamp swayed, and she steadied it.

Nick looked up, frowning, so that she did not go on. Her horror must have been written in her eyes, however, for he said roughly, "I'll do what I can, but I can't work miracles!"

"No, of course not. It is only that . . . he is so very young!"

"So are you—too young to be a party to this!"

"You cannot send me away now!" She willed herself to hold the lamp steady and tried not to think of Batty with only one arm for the rest of his life . . . if indeed he had a life! Somehow, the awful possibilities, once raised, seemed determined to take a permanent hold in her mind. If it came to the worst, she must endeavor not to be squeamish . . . How would the grisly task be accomplished, she wondered, teeth clenched. Would Captain Bannion cleave through the limb with one shattering blow, or must it be sawn off like a branch from a tree . . . ? There was a red mist before her eyes . . . the lamp began to sway wildly . . .

"Consuelo!" His voice came sharply but, from a long way off. "The devil! This is madness."

"No!" She dragged her thoughts back from the

unspeakable depths of her imagination. "I am all right."

"Very well, but we'll have one thing clear—if I can't save the arm, you'll have to leave. Understand? No arguments."

Consuelo nodded, relieved to have the decision taken out of her control.

As he worked she was hardly aware of the passage of time; her whole attention was fixed upon his hands, square capable hands with rather spatulate fingers that manipulated the displaced bone with an instinctive sureness, easing it with infinite care back into position until the two edges came together, grating slightly as they met. "Thank God it was a clean break," he muttered, lining up the piece of board he had brought in earlier with the arm and binding the two together swiftly and firmly. Only then did he straighted up, easing the cramp from his limbs.

"Well, that's it. I've done all I can. The rest is up to the Almighty—and Batty's constitution."

"Will he be all right?" Consuelo ventured half fearfully.

"The lad is young and strong; his bones should knit." Nick forced a measure of confidence into his voice. "Right, Joe, you can take him down to his own quarters, now."

"Oh, but wouldn't it be better if he remained here, and we could look after him?" She was still holding the lamp; indeed she was not sure if she could move her arm to set it down as she suddenly became aware of her own stiff sore body once more.

As Joe carried Batty away she found the lamp taken from her and Captain Bannion's arm firmly encircling her to keep her from falling. She winced involuntarily at his touch, and he frowned quite fiercely.

"You aren't looking after anyone except yourself from now on," he said with a strange huskiness in his voice that she couldn't quite understand. "You have already done more than your share, and in any case," he reasoned, forestalling the argument in her eyes, "the boy will be much happier among his own mates."

"Yes, I see." She was trying to concentrate, but his face kept growing fuzzy. It was really rather pleasant when he lifted her off her feet and carried her cradled high against his chest—like coming home. It reminded her of another time. . . . She yawned and smiled sleepily at him. "You are very gallant, señor . . . I am quite well able to walk, you understand, but . . ."

Her lashes fluttered down onto her cheeks and she was asleep before he left the room.

Chapter 12

Consuelo knew nothing of being carried to her bed, of Nick's murmured instructions to Maria to cover her with a blanket and let her sleep undisturbed, or of Lady Covington's less than enthusiastic reception of his display of concern.

She slept heavily and dreamlessly and awoke to find a thin wedge of sunlight striking in through the small aperture and prodding at her eyelids. Astonished to find herself still fully dressed, she instinctively made to sit up, a movement which brought an involuntary skirl of pain.

The sound had Maria hurrying to her side, and the maid's excitable, somewhat incoherent explanations and expressions of sympathy and admiration soon woke Lady Covington, who made her displeasure known in no uncertain manner.

"I am sorry, señora," said Consuelo with a sigh. "It was thoughtless of us to make so much noise. We shall try to remember—"

"My dear Consuelo, do not, I pray you, make an issue of it. I am fast becoming inured to inconvenience and discomfort. I console myself that this journey must come to an end before too much longer, and we may all return to a more civilized mode of

153

living." Verena arose and slipped on her peignoir, adding with gentle malice, "Unfortunately, my dear, unlike you, I shall be obliged to face the return journey before I can be truly at ease."

Her words, as they were meant to do, cast Consuelo into a profound depression. She did not wish to think of what was so soon to be and, to give her mind a new direction, fell instead to considering what Batty's condition might be this morning.

"You must help me to dress," she told Maria, swinging her legs stiffly down, "and then I may go and find out."

"Consuelo!" Verena Covington's voice was clipped with exasperation. "You will do no such thing." Consuelo turned to stare at her. "Until you are delivered safely into your father's care once more, I still consider myself to be in some sort responsible for you."

"Well, you need not," said Consuelo, drawing herself erect. "For Captain Bannion has made it very clear that I am *his* responsibility."

"To ensure your safe return, perhaps; but I was thinking more of your behavior . . ."

"You find my behavior in some way objectionable?" In spite of her extreme youth and her disheveled dress, there was an austere dignity about Consuelo that took Verena a little by surprise. She frowned and moderated her tone to that of the wise counselor.

"Not objectionable, my dear. I am sure you could never be *that*. Shall we say—a little too impulsive. It can be a charming characteristic in many ways, but when it leads one to be unwise . . ."

"How . . . unwise?"

A faint, half-pitying smile touched Verena's lips. "Well, you have been making rather a nuisance of yourself, have you not? Putting yourself in Captain

Bannion's way, distracting him from his duties—and then that ridiculous business last night . . ."

Consuelo swallowed hard. "Has he said that I have been a nuisance?"

"Not in so many words. But he took supper with us last night, and something that he said then did just make me wonder if you had not become something of an embarrassment to him!" Her voice was persuasive. "Only consider, my dear, how it must appear to his crew—to have an eager young girl forever hanging on his coattails!"

Was that how she had appeared? Consuelo flinched at the picture presented by Lady Covington. "Yes, I see," she said politely. "Thank you for telling me."

"You should not listen to her," Maria whispered angrily as she helped Consuelo into her dress. "Jealous as a cat, that one is, lady or no!"

"Hush, Maria!" Consuelo was abrupt with her. "You must not speak so. It is not seemly in you!"

"If you say so, señorita." The maid's expression was mulish. "But I can use my eyes, same as the next person," she muttered, "and it's plain to see—"

"Be quiet, I tell you! I will not be disobeyed!"

A look at her young mistress's face was enough to quell further argument, but Maria harbored her thoughts nonetheless.

It seemed that with the passing of the storm, the weather had taken a definite turn for the better and looked to be set fair for good sailing, with blue skies and a warm, stiffish breeze.

Henry had quite recovered his spirits and was eager to spend more time on deck to make up for lost time. It was Consuelo who now showed reluctance and had to be coaxed into the fresh air.

"Are you feeling quite well, señorita?" Mr. Fletcher

inquired when she declined to take any luncheon. "Not suffering any ill-effects from your accident, perhaps?"

She watched Lady Covington, her cloak billowing in the breeze as she laughed at some remark of Captain Bannion's. It seemed to her that they were looking her way. "No, I thank you," she said in a small voice. "I am just not hungry."

"Young Batty was asking after you this morning," Mr. Fletcher continued.

"Oh, how is he?" Animation momentarily lit her face.

"In a fair deal of discomfort, as yet, but we'll soon have him bobbing back like a cork I shouldn't wonder." Bob Fletcher grinned. "He's taken quite a shine to you, you know; telling anyone who'll listen that you are the nearest thing to an angel he's likely to see this side of heaven!"

"Goodness! There's an accolade, to be sure!" Lady Covington's trill of laughter announced her arrival on the scene. Captain Bannion was still with her. A faint flush stole into Consuelo's cheeks as she murmured that she had done very little.

"You won't convince Batty of that," said Nick, subjecting her to a searching scrutiny that left him puzzled. "Or me, for that matter," he added gently, and watched the flush deepen as her eyes flew to his. "You performed your part nobly."

"Maybe," said Henry in a mildly aggrieved way. "And as a result she is now quite done in!"

"No, I am not," Consuelo said crossly, moving away to stare blindly out over the rail. "I just wish for a little peace."

Behind her she heard Henry asking how long it would be before they arrived in Bilbao and Captain Bannion replying that if the present conditions prevailed, one more day should suffice. A lump rose in her throat. She tried to swallow it back and wondered if it would be terribly wicked to pray for another storm to blow them off course and thus prolong the journey.

"Do you feel up to trying your hand with the sextant again, Consuelo?"

His voice made her jump. Her heart leaped. And then she remembered Lady Covington's words: "You have been making rather a nuisance of yourself, have you not?" He was simply being kind. She said without turning round: "Thank you, señor, but I think perhaps Enrique was right; I am a little tired."

"Yes, of course." His voice assumed a more impersonal tone. "You had much better rest."

He strode away, and she was left with her confused emotions. "Where has my happy little Consuelo gone?" Enrique had chided her earlier, and she could not answer him. She looked back and marveled at that girl she had been in Brighton, so young and carefree and . . . light-minded! With every mile that took them closer to Spain, she felt that girl slipping away.

In her place was a young woman whose traitorous heart leaped not for Enrique, in whom she had reposed all her girlish adoration, but for another: a man different from Enrique in every possible way, a man who so plainly saw her as nothing more than an amusing and sometimes troublesome child. A great aching void filled her chest, and the waves blurred and danced before her eyes. If this was love, she wanted no part of it!

For the remainder of the journey she endeavored to be cheerful and to devote herself to Enrique, who did not deserve to be treated so shabbily. But it was not easy. It was as though the nearer she came to home, the more the mere thought of her father began to exert its influence over her; a kind of fatalism grew in her that he would not let her marry anyone but Don Miguel.

Too soon the schooner was into the Bay of Biscay and heading for Bilbao, already visible as a tiny huddle of houses, dwarfed by the might of the Pyrenees, peak upon peak stretching awesomely back into the misty distance and marching westward to join the Asturias.

In spite of herself and how little she had wished to return, the sight of this land to which she belonged touched some chord deep inside her. It was impossible to look upon such imposing grandeur and remain unmoved. Henry Linton acknowledged himself to be much impressed.

They sailed in past the small island of Santa Clara, the walls of its battle-scarred fort already growing over with lichen. But not so San Sebastian on its rocky promontory; jutting out into the bay. It bore mute evidence of the savage battering it had received in the closing stages of the war, the town's great fortress of La Mota on its great conical rock a ruined shell, the slender isthmus that connected it to the mainland a mass of rubble.

Consuelo's father had kept her closely confined within doors at that time, but she had heard the ceaseless pounding of the guns and the occasional sounds of shouting carried by the wind, and she had longed with all of a twelve-year-old's ardor to see the men of Wellington's glorious army drive the last of the French from her country. It was more than two whole weeks before she had been able to persuade Señora Diaz to take her in the carriage to view the devastated town.

Until that moment she had thought war a fine

gallant affair, but the sight of San Sebastian's principal street reduced to a heap of blackened rubble—its pretty arched gateway destroyed, the only sign of life among the ruins an odd haggard figure searching for belongings among the desolation—had filled her with a horror that caused her to wake screaming from nightmares for weeks afterward.

"You are very quiet, Consuelo. Such a pensive profile!" Captain Bannion had come up beside her at the rail. She turned slowly, reluctantly, to meet his eyes. "Not worrying, I trust?"

She shook her head. "I was remembering the battle. Were you here—at the end?"

"During the bombardment? Yes, I was here—or rather, I was up there." In a gesture that seemed perfectly natural he put an arm about her shoulders to turn her around a little; a faint tremor ran through her, but she made no attempt to move away as he pointed with the other hand. "You see that second ridge, the one with the curious bump? Well, there is a narrow pass there, undetectable until you are almost upon it, and if you follow it through and up it brings you out on the landward side where there is an amazing kind of castellated fortress built high into the face of the rock. It was from there that we used to sweep down to harry the retreating French."

As he spoke Henry came up to join them. He looked rather pointedly at the captain's familiar hold upon his affianced, and Nick, without undue haste or embarrassment, released her, his expression enigmatic.

"You spoke of 'we'?" Henry said. "Were you a special unit of Wellington's army?"

"No." Nick grinned almost boyishly, remembering. "Just me, and the most black-visaged group of brigands this land ever spawned! Their leader was a personable rogue known to all as *El Terremoto*—and a veritable 'earthquake' he could be, as I found to my cost on more than one occasion."

"Lord! It must have been the greatest adventure ever!" Henry exclaimed, eyeing his host with new respect.

"It was an experience, certainly," Nick said wryly. "But one I feel no strong urge to repeat."

Behind them Mr. Fletcher had been bawling out orders, and men were scrambling everywhere, hauling in sail, making ready to leap for the small quay to secure the mooring ropes. It might have been supposed that Nick had taken very little interest in the proceedings, but Consuelo saw that very little escaped his notice.

She hoped that he had been less observant about the effect his nearness had upon her. Beneath the fineness of the white muslin dress she wore, her skin still seemed to feel the imprint of his touch. It had taken every ounce of resolution not to lean against him as he stood so close beside her in that spontaneous gesture of intimacy.

"Consuelo, my dear, you are not wearing your bonnet." Verena Covington had come up on deck, having been informed by an excited Maria that they had arrived. She was looking coolly elegant in a walking dress of palest green twilled silk trimmed with blond ribbons and a hat with a large brim to shade her eyes and shield her flawless skin from the sun's rays.

She regarded the erect little figure in the simple white gown with a tinge of irritation. There was no way Consuelo could match her for style or elegance of dress or manner, yet there was a youthful dignity, a grace about her—in the way she held her head, perhaps, with its black hair as smooth and sleek as a little page boy's now that the ragged ends were becoming less apparent—which set Verena all at odds with herself and sharpened her voice. The sooner the child was out of her sight, the better. "It cannot be good for you to expose yourself so," she continued, investing the words with added meaning, so that Consuelo turned slightly widened eyes upon her and colored faintly. "Do go and ask Maria for your bonnet, there's a good girl. We shall be going ashore very soon, I expect."

Taking the girl's compliance for granted, she turned to Nick. "Well, Nicholas, how are we to proceed now that we have arrived?" Her eyes rested with distaste on the hot dusty quayside where a spavined mule slumbered uneasily between the shafts of a shabby cabriolet. "The place looks deserted. Does Señor Vasquez live far away?"

"About two miles along the Vitoria road." Nick was also eyeing the only visible means of transport with mixed feelings. One part of him wanted to get the whole thing over and finished—and to that end, the cabriolet offered the quickest solution, if the mule was equal to the journey, which he doubted. Nor would it carry them all. He sighed.

"I had better dispatch a messenger to the house. Señor Vasquez can then send his carriage for us."

"Well, thank the Lord for that," Henry said with a grin that concealed his growing nervousness now that the moment of confrontation had almost arrived. "I'd not fancy trusting myself to that bone-shaking contraption, I can tell you!"

Consuelo, coming back with reluctant steps, her charming poke bonnet dutifully tied, saw them all laughing together and was loath to join them. She saw a familiar jaunty figure sitting cross-legged atop of the nearest hatch, his splinted arm resting gingerly across his knees. She hurried across to him. "Batty! Oh, I

am pleased to have seen you before I left! How is
your poor arm?"

The boy's face split from ear to ear. "It'll do well
enough, miss—thanks to you," he said shyly.

"Oh, I didn't do very much. It is Captain Bannion
who must merit your thanks. He was quite splendid!"

"Oh, aye; the cap'n's a good man, right enough."
Batty blushed scarlet. "But I'd like to thank you
anyways."

Consuelo smiled and then, hearing some activity
ashore, looked up in time to see her father's carriage
rattling along the quayside, the horses coming to rest
at last almost eye to eye with the startled mule.

She bade Batty good-bye and hurried forward to
join the others. Captain Bannion was already ashore,
speaking to the driver. It was not Pedro, who had
been in her father's service forever, but a younger-
looking man. It was not surprising that Pedro had
been replaced, for he must have been very old, but
she had ever been a favorite with him and his absence brought an added sadness to her.

Enrique took her hand for reassurance—whether
his or hers she wasn't sure, "Well, Consuelo dearest,
this is it," he said, overheartedly. "I only hope your
papa don't refuse me admittance!"

Verena threw him an impatient look, but Consuelo
was more kind, saying, "I am sure he will see you,
querido. . . ." as she watched Captain Bannion swing
himself aboard once more, his shirt billowing in the
breeze, his manner purposeful. How pleased he must
be to have his task all but accomplished.

"Your father has had a man watching the bay each
day this past week," he said, making his way to her
side, "so that news of our arrival could be conveyed
to him at once. Hence the carriage."

Sailors were already bringing out the baggage and

taking it ashore to be stowed in the carriage, but the sheer volume of the load precipitated an altercation between them and the driver, which involved much flailing of arms and brought one of the men scurrying back to the ship with the news that there was insufficient room for so many boxes—a wagon must be sent later for the remainder. It was decided that Maria would remain to supervise their safe bestowal.

The moment could be delayed no longer. Consuelo took a last wistful look around at the schooner's deck, said a subdued good-bye to Mr. Fletcher, who wished her well in his shy way, and went ashore.

It was for the most part a silent journey, the occupants of the carriage being individually preoccupied with their own thoughts. Only when the ground became uncomfortably bumpy did Consuelo look out to find that they had left the road and were being driven over a rough track.

She threw a startled glance at Nick, who had at the same moment noticed that something was wrong. He leaned out of the window to shout to the driver, but his summons seemed only to galvanize the man into further excess; he whipped the horses into a frenzy, which sent them hurtling across the ground, bouncing over boulders with a force that only the superb springing of the carriage enabled them to withstand.

Nick, flung off balance, fell back, cutting his forehead on the side of the window as he did so; Verena Covington screamed loud and long and clung frantically to the rich plush hangings; Henry banged on the roof and demanded querulously to know what the devil the driver thought he was about, while Consuelo, heedless of the hideous jolting, sat transfixed by the sight of the dark stain that slowly spread and trickled down Captain Bannion's cheek.

"Señor—you are hurt! Your face—it is bleeding!"

Nick touched it briefly, then took out a handkerchief and pressed it over the cut.

"Is there n-nothing you can do!" sobbed Verena
Covington, her beautiful hat knocked askew, unbri-
dled terror in her eyes. "Before we are all k-killed!"

"Nothing," said Nick. "Until this madman decides
to call a halt to this crazy ride, there is nothing any of
us can do."

Just when it seemed that the springs would take
no more punishment, the pace slowed dramatically,
the whole vehicle turned around, rocking ominously,
and came finally to rest amid a cloud of dust.

For a moment nobody moved. Then Nick eased
himself painfully to his feet and opened the carriage
door. The cloud began to settle and from beyond it
appeared some half a dozen men in a ragbag assortment of clothes, an ominously silent semicircle which
closed in, brandishing musket and knife with an air
of purpose.

Chapter 13

"Where are we? What is happening? For God's sake, Nicholas, why don't you say something?" Lady Covington's voice teetered on the edge of hysteria.

It seemed a long time before he answered. "I can't answer for the exact location, but I very much fear we have been kidnapped." Her gasp went unheeded as his glance went from face to face of the men before him. Several were very young, but a couple he recognized. "I can even hazard a guess by whom," he said with astonishing calmness, meeting the broad surprised grin on one of the brigands. "What I am less sure about is why?"

"Señor Nicholas, is it really you?" crowed one of the men jubilantly. "How overjoyed El Terremoto will be when he discovers!"

"His joy will be short-lived if this nonsense doesn't stop here," Nick replied in his most clipped, authoritative voice. "If El Terremoto is now reduced to attacking innocent travelers, I can only exhort him to be more careful in his choice of victim, in the future. And now, if you please, we are pressed for time and are expected, so I would be obliged if you will stand aside and allow us to proceed."

Even as he spoke, Nick realized that this was no

random encounter. The driver had either been bribed or replaced. The general amusement among the group seemed to confirm that he was right. The brigands pressed closer, intrigued by the two tense but beautiful visions faintly visible through the dusty windows, and Nick, his mind working furiously, became aware of a scuffling behind him.

Henry, with some confused idea of escaping and going for help, had got the other door open and was down the steps and away before Nick could prevent him. With an oath Nick plunged after him, the driver shouted a warning to his compatriots, and there was a confused crackle of musket and pistol as several of the young brigands, overzealously ran around the back of the vehicle to pursue the escapees.

Consuelo was out of the carriage in an instant, heedless of Lady Covington's screams that she would be killed, and was running, stumbling over the ground to where Captain Bannion had pitched forward and now lay very still on the ground with Enrique bending over him, ashen-faced and trembling.

"I d-didn't mean . . ." he gasped. "Oh, God, I . . . j-just thought t-to get help, you know . . . he shouldn't have followed me!"

"It does not matter about that, now!" Consuelo was already on her knees, pushing aside the Captain's coat where a jagged tear was even now becoming stained with red, ripping open the shirt beneath to expose the wound in his side, which oozed blood steadily. With fumbling fingers she tore off his neck-cloth and folded it into a pad to press over the wound, exhorting Enrique to remove his also. "Quickly, I beg of you! And fold it."

As he complied shakily he was pushed aside by the man the captain had called Paco, who fell on to his knees beside Consuelo.

"*Caramba!*" he muttered, shaking his head. "That such a thing should happen! These young hotheads . . . El Terremoto will be very angry . . . he was as a brother to the Señor Nicholas!"

"Be silent, *estupido,*" she said, clenching her teeth to stop their chattering. "Try instead if you cannot contrive to be of use! The captain is not dead yet, nor will he be if we do not allow it. He would be better turned a little on to his side, I think, and we must have something soft for a pillow. Enrique?"

She turned to find him at her shoulder, looking down with something like despair. Her hand with the pad was still pressed firmly to the wound, but the blood was seeping through between her fingers and the white muslin of her skirt was stained bright red. He was very pale as she took the folded neckcloth from him.

"Please, mi Enrique, do not look like that! Captain Bannion is not going to die!"

It was defiantly said. She was frightened and fighting panic. She wished very much to succumb to hysterics like Lady Covington, but pride would not permit it, and besides there was no time. She swallowed convulsively to quell the rising nausea and resolutely applied her mind to necessities. The flow of blood had eased a little, but it was obvious that a neckcloth was quite inadequate.

"We must have something larger," she announced. "Enrique, you must go and fetch fresh linen—shirts or dresses—yes, there are plenty of muslin dresses in my portmanteaux! Oh, hurry, *please.*"

She was too engrossed to notice the strange glance he gave her. Paco attempted to stop him and she turned on the bandit a stream of Spanish that made him blink and withdraw his objections, though one of the young men went with Lord Linton.

While they were gone, Paco, much impressed by Consuelo's resourcefulness, turned the Señor Nicholas on his side as she had stipulated and, removing his own jacket, folded it and put it beneath his head. The cut on the forehead had opened up again with the fall and was seeping slightly, which served to emphasize his pallor. It did not bode well, Paco thought, but had wisdom enough not to say so.

Soon Henry Linton returned with his arm full of dresses and shirts and more neckcloths, which he said could be tied together to bind the pad in place—a suggestion which earned him a word of praise from his beloved. Also he had brought a flask of brandy.

Less welcome was Lady Covington, who had been discovered still in the coach by the bold-eyed young brigand. She watched impassively as Consuelo folded a dress and tied it up in a shirt to make a large firm pad which Henry then bound into place as tightly as possible. They tried to force a little brandy between his lips, but without success.

"You are wasting your time," she said with an air of one who has abandoned all hope.

"And you know nothing of the matter," Consuelo retorted angrily. "And are quite unfeeling, besides . . . It is my belief that Señor Bannion struck his head again as he fell and that is why he is unconscious. He will recover very soon, you will see."

Verena gave a tight little laugh. "It makes little difference. These creatures will probably kill us all anyway!"

"Oh, no! This has all been a great mistake. This man"—she indicated Paco—"knows Señor Bannion. I heard him say so."

Paco, not knowing what was being said of him but judging it from her deameanor to be complimentary, nodded eagerly, showing a great many uneven teeth in a wide grin.

Consuelo stood up stiffly, cast a vague uncertain look at her stained hands, and proceeded to wipe them on her skirt, which was already past saving. She ignored Verena's exclamation of horror and turned to Paco.

"And now, señor, if you will be so good as to have Captain Bannion carried to the coach, we must take him back to Bilbao with all speed so that Dr. Moreno, who has been our family physician for many years, may remove the ball that is lodged in his side and tend him until he is well."

There was a curious little silence, during which the soughing of the wind seemed to mock at her. For the first time she became aware of their total isolation. The clearing in which they stood was at the mouth of a canyon cut in to the towering mountains; the path along which they had come disappeared into a dense area of woodland and scrub. A small frisson of fear crawled up her neck, though she adopted her most haughty manner.

"Well?"

Paco looked unhappy. "I regret, Señorita Vasquez, that what you ask is impossible."

His use of her name jolted her into recognizing what until now she had been too distraught to consider seriously. There had been no mistake. How these men had come by her father's carriage she did not care to contemplate, but all that had happened had been carefully planned. Enrique, not understanding what was being said, but very much aware of the sudden tensions, came to stand at her shoulder, demanding in a low voice to know what was going on.

"In a moment, *querido*," she said without taking

her eyes off Paco. It was an effort to keep her voice
steady. "What do you mean—impossible?"

Paco spread his hands. The others grouped about
him, menacing once more, their weapons very much
to the fore.

"El Terremoto is even now expecting us, and notwithstanding the risk to the Señor Nicholas's health,
only a big fool attempts to cross El Terremoto!" He
saw that she was about to argue. "Please, señorita; it
is of no use!"

"Why does this great man that you speak of not
come to do his own kidnapping? Very brave! To
leave it all to others!"

"Not so. He was not able—"

"He means to demand a ransom of my father, does
he not?"

Paco was looking harassed. "That is not for me to
say," he muttered evasively. "No, no, señorita! No
more. We have wasted much time already! Soon it
will be evening, and we must go from here on foot.
Heh, Miguel . . . Fernando, you will fashion some
form of litter to render the Señor's journey as comfortable as possible."

The men looked disgruntled. "How are we to do
that?"

"How? I do not know how! Use the few brains God
gave you and do not expect me to do everything for
you!" He turned back to Consuelo, who was explaining matters to Enrique somewhat incoherently. "For
you, señorita, we have a mule." His glance moved
nervously to the sullen beauty with the red-gold
hair. "Had we known, we would have brought two."

Consuelo was swift to seize the opportunity. "Well
then, it is simple," she coaxed. "Since it is me you
want, you can let my friends go. They will be noth-

ing but a hindrance to you, and they may then take
Captain Bannion back in the carriage to Bilbao. . . ."

He put back his head and laughed. "Señorita, I
like you! You have a quick wit and much generosity
of spirit! But no, your friends, they have seen too
much. We will go all together, I think."

She gave up. She was hot and tired, and there was
dust in her throat and eyes, making them feel gritty
and sore. Enrique would have argued further, but
she dissuaded him, feeling quite unequal to the task
of interpreting.

They went instead to join Lady Covington, who
had found a convenient rock with some degree of
shade upon which to rest; the bold-eyed young brig-
and had been persuaded to fetch her parasol from
the carriage and was hovering nearby in open admiration. Already the older woman had recovered
some of her poise, and this had the effect of making
Consuelo feel hotter and grubbier than ever.

"My dear child, you look quite dreadful! Doesn't
she, Henry? Surely even these barbarians would not
object to your changing that awful gown?" Verena's
pitying tone aroused a stubbornness in Consuelo.

"I do not mind." She shrugged.

"Well, perhaps you do not." A strident note crept
into the voice. "But you might, out of simple courtesy,
consider the feelings of others."

"Verena, stop it." Henry took Consuelo's arm. "You
do indeed look weary, my dear—and small wonder!
Come and sit down." He told Verena the gist of what
Consuela had told him.

"But that is monstrous!" she cried. "Have you
looked about you? We cannot possibly be expected
to walk!"

The terrain was indeed formidable. Consuelo's heart
sank at the thought of what lay ahead, but it was the

effect the journey would have upon Captain Bannion that most exercised her mind.

"You may have the mule," she said absently. "I shall walk."

"Thank you!" said Verena Covington with crushing sarcasm that went largely unnoticed. "But I fail to see why we should be expected to go anywhere. It is quite obviously *you* that they want. . . ."

"Verena!"

Consuelo said wearily, "I have already explained that to Paco, but he will not listen."

"Well, I, for one, would not think of leaving you to cope alone," said Henry nobly, glaring across at Verena.

Consuelo smiled and touched his arm. "Thank you, *querido*. It is good of you to say it."

"I mean it," Henry said, and was surprised to find that he did mean it.

With little choice but to comply, the party was soon ready to leave. Miguel and Fernando had in the end contrived a more comfortable litter than might have been expected by the simple expedient of tearing out one of the carriage seats and securing it to a pair of stout young tree branches with the torn-up pieces of Henry's shirt. To this, Captain Bannion was firmly tied with more strips of linen.

He was showing signs of returning consciousness as they set out, which had the effect of lightening Consuelo's step considerably, though he seemed very confused as to what was happening.

Henry managed to get him to swallow a little brandy, and for a moment his eyes moved restlessly over the scene, finally coming back to Henry. He said faintly, but with perfect clarity, "Look after Consuelo. . . ." And then his concentration wavered.

"Go back to sleep and do not worry," Consuelo

told him fiercely over a lump in her throat. "I will not let them jolt you if it can be avoided!"

He frowned, not understanding, but her voice seemed to reassure him and he closed his eyes again.

After a while, she lost all sense of time. They trudged along together, she and Enrique, close to the litter, his hand always ready to aid her if she stumbled, or if, as sometimes happened, the mule ahead of them slipped, sending a shower of loose stones down upon them. Poor Enrique, she thought. He was very much disheveled. There was little now remaining of that fashionable image so dear to him . . . and yet she had never liked him better.

They seemed to be climbing up and up . . . and sometimes, as she lifted her head, she caught a glimpse of the bay glittering far below in the clear evening light.

And then, quite suddenly it seemed, they rounded a sheer rock face to be met with the strangest of sights, something part castle, part rock, which together created the most extraordinary illusion of grandeur. They were ushered through a cavelike entrance into a tiny courtyard open to the sky, and thence into a cavernous interior where the only natural light came from slits high up in the walls. From the great vaulted roof hung a massive circular lamp fashioned of intricate ironwork, which must surely have come from some Moorish palace.

A long refectory table occupied the center of the floor, and there was a general impression of shabby magnificence overall, if one could overlook the formidable array of weapons adorning the walls.

From a sofa draped with brilliant silk shawls a figure arose as they entered, supporting himself by means of a gold-headed cane. Consuelo thought that he was probably the most handsome man that she had ever seen—not overly tall, but superbly proportioned, and with a kind of vibrant animal grace which even a heavily bandaged foot could not diminish. She noticed glossy black hair curled tightly about the strong bronzed face and black eyes glinting with a beguiling insolence as she was led in, followed by Lady Covington, then Enrique—and lastly the litter bearing Captain Bannion.

"*Santa Maria, Madre de Dios!*" he exclaimed in a deep, amused voice. "Paco, my friend, what *have* you brought me?"

The black eyes, which had marked and recognized Consuelo's presence, passed over Henry Linton with no more than a faint query and came to dwell with wicked speculation upon Verena Covington, who in spite of being cross and tired and decidedly disheveled, still managed to exude a certain allure. And notwithstanding that she felt grossly ill used, she recognized that look for what it was and knew a curious little thrill of anticipation.

"Ladies! I am honored!" he exclaimed jovially. "Come and sit. You must be distressed by fatigue after such a tiresome journey. I make you my apologies for the necessity which prompted it."

Verena swept past him and sank onto the sofa. "You are too kind!" she murmured with gentle sarcasm as she leaned back, looking up to meet his eyes. "I hope you mean to explain that necessity to my satisfaction, for I tell you plainly I do not intend to remain here a moment longer than I must!"

His eyebrow lifted with comic surprise, and he was on the point of replying when his attention was diverted. He had paid little heed to the litter when it was brought in and set down upon a large couch against the wall; only as the occupant groaned and Consuelo rushed forward to kneel beside it did he swing himself across with the aid of his stick to take a closer look.

As he recognized his erstwhile comrade and took in his condition, he swore a great oath. His rumbling voice filled the cavern as he turned to fix each of his men in quick succession with eyes suddenly hardened to a dangerous glitter.

"Who is responsible for this?" he demanded softly, but it was the menacing softness of thunder on the verge of explosion. "Point out to me the miserable cur and I, El Terremoto, will personally cut him into little pieces and serve him up to the fishes in the bay!"

There was an uneasy silence broken by a weary chuckle. "I see that time has not succeeded in blunting the more colorful excesses of that blistering tongue!" It was Nick's voice, sounding weak, but blessedly normal.

Consuelo gasped with relief and promptly burst into tears.

Chapter 14

In a small turret chamber above the great cavernous hall, Consuelo sat as she had done for most of the past two days beside the couch upon which Captain Bannion lay sleeping, a natural healing sleep at last after the hours of feverish tossing.

It had been the strangest experience, full of conflicting impressions—of this fortress where nothing was quite as one might expect, and of El Terremoto himself, an overpowering man whose moods could swing from gentleness and charm to towering rage and back again in a matter of moments, a man who with a swaggering display of arrogance had boasted that they were indeed his prisoners, yet very soon afterward had acted with commendable swiftness and with the skill of a surgeon to remove the bullet lodged in Captain Bannion's side.

It had tried her fortitude severely to witness this delicate operation, but a deep suspicion of his ability to carry it off successfully made her presence imperative, despite all of Enrique's protestations that it was not seemly, nor indeed wise.

Her insistance did not, however, as Henry had feared, goad the brigand chief to anger; rather he seemed to view her determination with a kind of indulgent admiration, and he assured her gravely at the end of his operation that no vital organ had been damaged.

"You are sure?" insisted Consuelo, very pale.

"It is certain. Nick has lost much blood, it is true, and there may be some fever, but"—he grinned, showing strong white teeth—"I tell you, chiquita, this old comrade of mine has come through worse things! He has the constitution of a *toro bravo* and will soon recover."

"*Si Dios quiere!*" she murmured on a sob.

"Naturally." He gave her a curious look. "But why should God withhold his will from such a fine man? You should have more faith, little one."

"Yes, you are right," she said, pulling herself together and finding something strangely comforting and not the least offensive in being addressed so familiarly by this man who made no bones about having kidnapped her for ransom.

"Of course I am right," he assured her, "And now, Paco is going to supervise Nick's removal to a chamber upstairs that has been prepared for him, and you and your companions will take supper with me."

"Oh, but . . ."

"See, your friend waits," he said, amused, indicating Henry, who had remained doggedly throughout the ordeal, though well out of view of the actual operation, to see that she came to no harm. "The portmanteaux have been brought up from the carriage so that you may change that soiled dress for a fresh one."

She looked down as if surprised to see what a sorry picture she presented. "Yes, of course, but I am not hungry, you know, and would much prefer to remain with Captain Bannion."

El Terremoto chuckled. "What a fierce little pro-

tector Nicholas has in you! But I have given him a
powerful draft and he will not stir for some time, I
promise you! And Paco has orders to watch him like
a mother hen! Come now," he coaxed. "You will not
allow the beautiful Lady Covington to outshine you?
She is already adorning herself if I have not mis-
judged her!"

Consuelo wanted to say that she cared nothing for
that, but sensed that there was little point in arguing
further, and besides, Enrique was growing restless.

Supper was a strange meal—and a surprisingly
palatable one—of chicken cooked in some special
way with herbs, and served at the richly laid refectory table by a sullen beauty whom El Terremoto
addressed casually as Juanita. From her attitude it
soon became clear that she was his woman and deeply
resented their presence, especially that of Lady
Covington, who, for all her bitter complaints, had
decked herself out with considerable care in her
finest gown and was not averse to a little oblique
flirtation with the handsome brigand chief, who responded with obvious enjoyment.

Henry, once more restored to his former elegance,
was very quiet. The formality of the meal had taken
him by surprise; the quality of the wine made his
eyebrows lift—doubtless, it had been dishonestly
acquired—and the affability of his captor stuck in his
throat more than somewhat. But it was Consuelo's
behavior that most exercised his mind.

She had remained preoccupied, no more than toying
with her food, even when El Terremoto had dis-
cussed the size of the ransom he would be asking, an
amount that made Henry blink, without the least
hint of awkwardness or regret. Only once did she lift
her head, white-faced, and that was when he an-

nounced that Don Miguel Alphonso de Aranches was
even now at Señor Vasquez's villa.

"One must be realistic, my friends," El Terremoto
explained urbanely, noting Henry's reaction. "Both
gentlemen are exceedingly wealthy, and both will
undoubtedly pay much to ensure that the little señorita
is returned to them unharmed." He smiled, seeming
thus to emphasize rather than diminish the threat
implicit in his words. "My terms will be delivered to
the villa"—a pause here, for effect—"soon."

"How soon?" Henry demanded.

The brigand's smile deepened. "When they have
had time to sweat a little over your disappearance."

"And if your demands are not met?" Verena's voice
grew a trifle shrill. "What then?"

"Please!" He put up a hand, clearly enjoying himself.
"Let us not spoil an excellent meal by contemplating
unpleasant possibilities. My digestion, you understand,
does not permit."

Having witnessed the way he wolfed down his
food, Verena thought this highly improbable and, in
her agitation, was so unwise as to say as much. "I
vow you must have the digestion of an ox!"

At once the atmosphere cooled. The handsome
black brows drew together and she felt Henry tense
beside her. Only Consuelo seemed unaware that anything was amiss. Really, the child must be totally
lacking in sensitivity, as she had more than once
suspected, and did not deserve consideration. But
for herself, she concluded belatedly, it had been a
mistake to bait the Spaniard. She bit her lip and
resorted to one of her more powerful weapons—guile.

"Surely, señor"—she pouted prettily—"you must
be aware of my . . . distress at not knowing what is to
become of me! I have become embroiled, in all

innocence, in a situation which has very little to do with me. . . ."

Eyes narrowed, El Terremoto considered her over the rim of his glass, elbows propped casually on the table. "But, are you not then the friend, the chaperon, of Señorita Vasquez?"

Again Verena saw her mistake. It was not like her to be so careless. She fought down her impatience and the fear that clamored to hold sway. His initial attraction remained curiously undiminished, but her fear of him grew. She sensed that he set great store by loyalty in the stupid way that men so often did, and that she would get nowhere with him by appearing merely self-interested.

"Yes, of course!" She infused the right amount of warmth, of pleading, into her voice. "Consuelo is a dear girl. I am devoted to her. Surely you must see that it is my concern for her, even more than for myself, which prompts my every thought!"

"Quite so," he said dryly. "such selflessness is naturally touching, señora! But we will not cross any bridges until there is need."

And with that, Lady Covington had to be content.

Consuelo, for her part, welcomed the end of the meal, when she had at last been permitted to take up her place where she most wished to be—at Captain Bannion's side—to wait anxiously for some spark of returning consciousness.

Later in the evening, El Terremoto came stomping up the winding turret stairs with the aid of his stick. "Well, and how is our brave comrade, heh?" he boomed, his presence filling the tiny room.

"He has stirred a little, and once he muttered something, but I could not quite hear. . . ." She strove to sound confident and practical. "That is good, don't you think?"

"Splendid!" He bent over the couch, laid a hand on Nick's forehead, lifted one eyelid and felt his pulse. "Splendid," he said again.

"I believe he should have some mulled wine when he does wake," she continued in a determined tone. "It is very good for fevers, I think. And perhaps a little later, some broth. That chicken we had for supper—the stock in which it was cooked would make an excellent broth. . . ."

El Terremoto was amused. "I will instruct Juanita to await your orders, señorita! Pray, do not fail to inform me if there is any further way in which I may be of service!"

The teasing inflection in his voice made her look up at him with an uncertain smile. "You do not really mind? He is your friend, after all."

"So he is," he agreed gravely. "And one to whom I owe much." After a significant pause, he said softly, "But what is he to you, I wonder?"

She averted her face, her voice so faint that he had to strain to hear it. "He . . . is my friend, also. He has been very kind."

"I see. And this Lord Linton who follows you with his eyes—is he also your friend? And what of Don Miguel, heh?" He chuckled at her embarrassment. "You would appear to be much in demand, little señorita!"

Consuelo tried to assert some kind of dignity. "It is a very complicated situation . . . and if you do not mind my saying so, none of your business. I prefer not to explain."

"You are wise," he agreed magnanimously. "Explanations are frequently tedious, and as such are better avoided!" At the door he said, "Useless for me to urge you to take your rest and let one of my men watch over Nicholas, I suppose? No? Then Paco will remain just beyond the door within call."

"There is no need . . ."

A soft rumbling laugh shook him. "For you, perhaps not." His eyebrow quirked irrepressibly. "But Nicholas might well have needs quite improper for a young lady to fulfill!"

"Oh!" She bit her lip, embarrassed once more. "I had not thought . . ."

He was still chuckling faintly as he left.

Henry came up soon afterward to try to persuade her to change her mind, but found her adamant.

"These men are so . . . crude," she explained lamely. "One could not trust them to know the right things to do."

"And you do, of course," he challenged her. And then, unable to deceive himself any longer about what was happening, he said involuntarily, "Consuelo . . . ?"

But Consuelo thought she had seen a movement from the couch and was bending forward eagerly. "Oh, Enrique, do you think . . . ?" And then, "No." She sighed and turned back to him. "I am sorry, *querido*. You were saying?"

"It doesn't matter!" he said shortly, the endearment grating suddenly on his ears. "It is easy to see that you have but one thing on your mind at present. I will relieve you of my company."

She was a little surprised by his shortness but supposed that he must be tired. And then she forgot about him altogether, for the captain was at last stirring, opening eyes that were heavy-lidded, vague, until at last they found hers.

"Consuelo?" He moved his hand across the blanket to take hers. "Damned silly, this." He frowned. "Did I imagine . . . ?"

"No," she said quickly to spare him the effort. "But it is all right. Your brigand friend has removed your bullet most efficiently!"

He smiled faintly and then with a groan closed his eyes. "Tell him . . . must let you go . . . at once."

"I think he will not do so, even to please you. And if he did, *amigo*, I would not go until you are well enough to go with me!" she insisted, watching him anxiously. Had he swooned away again, or simply gone to sleep? The slight pressure of his fingers on hers might almost have been imagined, as might the single word that came out on a breath: "*stubborn* . . ."

At first she was cheered by this brief exchange, but as time wore on he began to grow restless, muttering in his sleep, and when she smoothed the damp curling hair from his brow, she found it hot— much too hot. His hand reached up to grasp her wrist, his voice fretful: "Don't run from me . . . not again!" he said in a harried tone, though his eyes did not recognize her.

"Never, *querido mio*, I promise you!"

Consuelo's voice was unsteady. She felt desperately afraid all of a sudden. It had been so easy to show confidence, to declare her ability to look after him, but now she realized how woefully ignorant she was in such matters . . . and if he should die because she did the wrong thing, or equally as bad, failed to do the right thing? They were here in this terrible isolated place with no help to be had, and she knew that Lady Covington would be of little use—or Enrique. There was only one person to whom she *could* turn . . .

She was on her feet, calling for Paco, who came on the instant, looking sleepy. He must, she demanded, fetch El Terremoto at once.

"So what is the urgency?" grunted the chief, none too pleased to be torn from a most pleasurable diversion.

But one look at Nick's flushed and twitching face and he was bawling orders for water to be boiled and brought. For a considerable time an anxious silence reigned. El Terremoto busied himself applying fomentations while Consuelo found some relief for her apprehension in carefully sponging the captain's face with a cloth drenched in cool lavender water begged from Lady Covington, who relinquished it with an ill grace.

When they had accomplished all that could be accomplished, the two sat on together—a strange pair—Consuelo drawing unexpected comfort and strength from the brigand chief, who so obviously had a genuine affection for the captain.

Soon it became clear even to her eyes that their patient was easier. Paco, commanded by his chief, departed and returned presently with a jug of mulled wine and three glasses. Consuelo looked dubious as one was poured for her.

"Drink," said El Terremoto. "It will give you new strength." He took his own glass and saluted her.

She complied, sipping at first, wrinkling her nose as the hot strong liquid caught in her throat. But it did have a most beneficial effect. Her worries for Captain Bannion began to recede; if the wine might only have the same effect upon him . . . The torch-light was weaving fantastic shadows above his head; she felt light-headed and, turning to meet the brigand's eyes, found them curiously bright with . . . what? Satisfaction? A certain smugness? His face wavered with frightening irregularity, his teeth glinting in a broad smile as she tried—and failed—to rise to her feet.

"You . . . have . . . drugged me!" She mouthed the accusation with great difficulty, and was unsure whether the words had come out at all. But they must have, for his rumbling laugh seemed to fill her head, his voice coming from a long way off.

"A pity, little señorita. It was the only way!"

There was light coming from a slit high up in the wall. Consuelo lay staring at it for some moments as recollection returned. She was in the chamber alloted to Lady Covington and herself, but as to how she had got there . . . ?

"Well, so you are awake at last!" Lady Covington's voice was taut. "I thought you would sleep forever!"

Consuelo sat up abruptly and felt her head swim. She remembered the turret room, Captain Bannion in a fever—and the mulled wine. And now it was daylight. "How did I come here? And what time is it?"

"How?" Verena Covington's laugh had a brittle edge. "You were carried, my dear—by that awful bow-legged little man!"

"Paco?"

Verena shrugged. "I believe that is his name. As for the time, I have no idea. In this appalling tedium, time has little meaning. I suppose it must be midmorning."

"*Madre de Dios!*" Consuelo scrambled off the bed, disentangling herself from a riotous assortment of shawls. "Captain Bannion—I must find out how he is!"

"Really!" Verena exclaimed. "Consuelo, come back at once! You are behaving most foolishly. Have you no pride?"

"None!" came the echo of a reply.

No one tried to bar Consulo's way and soon she

was standing on the threshold of the room where Captain Bannion lay, her eyes turning irresistibly in his direction. How still he was. At his side, El Terremoto dozed in the chair with apparent unconcern. He stirred and came awake at her entrance.

"Well, little señorita, are you feeling more rested?"

She regarded him balefully. "You drugged me!"

He put back his head and laughed. "A simple potion to make you sleep. Admit that you are the better for it."

It was true, but she would not give him the satisfaction of knowing it. "I . . . that is not the point," she said with deliberate hauteur. "I would much have preferred to remain here."

"Believe me, *pobrecita,*" he said, not unkindly. "It was for the best. There was little you could have done."

A terrible fear clutched at her stomach. "He is not . . . ?"

"No! Nothing of the kind. Nicholas has won his battle against the fever some hours since and is now sleeping like a baby! Come," he said as she still looked disbelieving. "Lay your hand on his brow and you will see."

He hauled himself out of the chair and reached for his stick. "You may resume your vigil. I suppose you did not wait for breakfast? I will arrange something." His eyes twinkled. "I am sure that when Nicholas wakes, he would rather see your face than mine!"

"Thank you," she said, suddenly shy.

Chapter 15

When Nick opened his eyes and saw the turret room, he thought himself back in the war. There was a pain in his side that he felt too weary to investigate further; nor for the present was he even remotely curious as to its cause. This state of lethargy was not unpleasant and might have continued indefinitely had he not turned his head on the pillow.

There was a slim young girl in all the freshness of sprigged muslin, sitting beside his bed, her dark head bent in grave contemplation of her hands. As he moved she looked up swiftly and the last wreaths of slumber drifted from his brain.

"So it *was* you, Consuelo," he said faintly. "I didn't dream you, after all."

"No," she said, all the words she wanted to pour out locked in her throat. She moved to sit on the edge of the bed, looking at him intently.

He pushed one hand across the coverlet to meet hers, his fingers closing weakly round it. They were cool fingers, with no thread of fever remaining.

Tears filled her eyes soundlessly and spilled over. "You are better!"

His blue eyes crinkled into a semblance of their

former twinkle. "You don't seem very pleased about it."

She scrubbed impatiently at the tears with her free hand and smiled mistily at him. "Oh, but I am! It is very silly to cry when one is so happy! I must send word to El Terremoto; he also will be pleased."

There was a faint quirk of one eyebrow. "Ah, yes, that old rogue!"

"He saved your life," she said quickly, determined to be fair.

"Then I must be—and am—indebted to him." Nick frowned. "But that in no way alters the fact that *you* should not be here. I cannot permit him to continue to hold you against your will."

"Oh, please!" cried Consuelo. "You must not tease yourself with such matters now. You are still very weak."

"Now there I very much fear you are right." He sighed and closed his eyes.

"And truly, I do not mind being here, though I wish you might persuade your brigand friend to let the others go free."

"What? Are we all here, then?" His shoulders shook with silent laughter, which made him grimace and bite his lip. "Oh, God, what a ridiculous business!"

"That sounds like the comrade I remember!" said El Terremoto from the doorway. He limped across and took Nick's wrist between his fingers. A slow smile spread across his face. "Good. If you will only cease to excite yourself unnecessarily, we shall have you on your feet in no time!"

"Thanks largely to you, I'm told."

The smile became a chuckle. "And to your own personal nursemaid. Would that I might have so formidable an ally, should I ever be similarly placed!"

Nick turned his wrist to grip El Terremoto's hand

as the brigand was about to withdraw it. "As to that, we must talk, you and I."

The two men locked glances for a moment. "Very well. But just the two of us, eh?" The brigand turned to Consuelo. "Perhaps, señorita, you might go in search of some good nourishing broth for our patient?"

"Yes, of course." But she went reluctantly, not wanting her fate to be decided behind her back, not wanting to be separated for one moment longer than need from Captain Bannion.

In the great room below she found Enrique stretched out in a chair before a fitful fire. He sprang to his feet upon seeing her with rather more animation than was usual in him. Of Lady Covington there was no sign, the only other person in view being one of the brigands, who lounged against the far wall whiling away his spell of guard duty by whittling at a piece of wood in a halfhearted fashion.

Consuelo accosted him imperiously and demanded that he show her the way to the kitchens. A brief argument was waged before he shrugged and put away his knife.

His lordship watched the exchange with considerable impatience before saying a little testily, "From your demeanor, my dear, I infer that our gallant captain is on the road to recovery?"

She turned a shining face to him. "Yes! Is it not splendid? I am come to procure some broth for him."

He caught hold of her arm as she would have turned away. "Well, before you do . . . Oh, see here, Consuelo, send that fellow on ahead to the kitchen and listen to me for a moment!"

Something in his tone arrested her wandering thoughts. She did as he asked, looking up at him inquiringly.

"The thing is," he went on, "I have been getting to

know that Juanita girl rather well whilst you have
been preoccupied elsewhere. . . . He met her eyes a
shade defiantly. "Well, there hasn't exactly been a
lot else to do with Verena sulking in her room whenever that Terremoto fellow hasn't been around to
make sheep's eyes at!"

His remarks about Lady Covington no longer had
the power to shock her, but she did feel a measure of
guilt that he had been so neglected; he had not asked
to be kidnapped, after all, and a cavernous, uncomfortable fortress buried deep in the mountains could
hardly be accounted his milieu; it would be wonderful indeed if he did not feel a little out of sorts. She
swallowed her impatience to return to the turret
room and smiled kindly at him.

"I am truly sorry, *querido*, but . . ."

"Yes, I know; the captain's needs were greater
than mine!" He could not for the life of him keep the
sarcasm out of his voice, but before she could protest,
he had lowered his voice and was continuing. "Never
mind that now. Just listen to me before that man
comes back! Juanita is as jealous as a cat over Verena,
and is deucedly anxious to have us away from here.
To that end she is prepared to help us."

Consuelo stared at him, uncomprehending.

"Don't you see? She can drug the brigands' wine—
also, she knows where your father's coach and the
horses are hidden, in a small cave at the foot of these
mountains," he finished triumphantly. "The coach-
man is held there, too—and with only one man to
stand watch. He can be drugged like the rest, and
our escape will then be simple. Only consider, your
father will not have to pay El Terremoto one single
dollar! *That* ought to make him suitably grateful to
me, don't you think?"

She did not respond to his attempted quip, her

reaction being dismay. "But is this Juanita not afraid that El Terremoto will find out?" Consuelo shuddered. "*I* would not care to cross such a one!"

"She is willing to take that chance," he insisted. "She means to drink some of the wine herself when we have gone; that way he will suppose we have tampered with it."

"I think it is a stupid plan," she said flatly. "It will never succeed."

"Well, it's better than rotting here indefinitely." Henry was proving surprisingly stubborn. "Lord, Consuelo—I expected Verena to cavil, but not you! With your propensity for tumbling from one adventure to the next, I should have thought you'd leap at the chance." When she did not at once reply, he fell to coaxing. "Do say you'll come. We must decide so that arrangements can be made. We shall have to be ready to leave just before darkness falls this evening."

"Oh, but that is impossible! Captain Bannion will not be fit to undertake such a journey for several days!"

"I had not thought to take the captain along."

Consuelo's indignation rose. "*Insensato!* How can you be so ungrateful when he wounded himself to save you?"

"I'm not ungrateful! But if we wait, the whole purpose of attempting an escape is rendered useless! It isn't as though these people would harm him; why, dammit, they know him better than we do!"

"That is not the point!" Consuelo insisted doggedly.

"No." She heard his breath sucked in. His fingers fell from her arms as though they burned at the touch, and he swung away to stare down at the fire's feebly licking flames. "That much is fast becoming clear. The point being that I no longer take first place with you!"

Consuelo regarded his back, rigid with the hurt to his pride, and wanted desperately to ease that hurt. She went up to him and touched his arm. "*Querido,* you must know that I am very fond of you. . . ."

"But you are *in love* with Bannion." He completed the sentence for her, looking angrily aslant into her eyes. She went so pale that for a moment he thought that she might swoon. She didn't, yet her very stillness disturbed him almost as much, her enormous dark eyes seeming to dominate her face. "Are you all right, Consuelo?"

She was a long time answering. "Yes. Just . . . it was strange, hearing you say it like that. I have never attempted to put it into words."

He had to ask. "Is he in love with you?"

A tremor, as though of pain, shook her, but her voice was steady. "I do not think it."

The fool, thought Henry, and then tentatively, not attempting to touch her, he said, "Well then? Surely we can go on as we were? Perhaps my feelings for you have not always been of the deepest, but in this past week they have undergone a considerable change—and you have already admitted that you are fond of me. . . ."

She shook her head. "It can never again be as it was," she said with a sad little smile. "We are no longer the same two people, you and I."

"I could make you love me!"

Again she shook her head. "Such a love cannot be forced. It must be freely given without asking for anything in return."

He realized then what he should have seen before— that Consuelo had grown, almost overnight, it seemed, from a carefree girl into a deeply perceptive young woman. And he knew in that same moment that he had lost his chance with her forever.

*   *   *

When Consuelo returned to the turret room, she found Captain Bannion alone, and apparently asleep. But he opened his eyes as she set the tray down near the couch.

"Have I disturbed you?"

"No." He gave her a tired smile. "My eyelids seem weighted with lead and, in consequence, close upon the slightest provocation!"

El Terremoto had already propped him up with extra cushions. She perched a little self-consciously on the edge of the couch and took up the bowl.

"That smells good." His eyebrow quirked. "Are you going to spoon-feed me?"

She bit her lip shyly. "Shall you mind? If you would care to try if you can manage . . . ?"

"I doubt I could raise that much energy, my dear. I'm still as weak as a cat." There was a hint of a twinkle in his eye. "Besides, what man in his right mind would put himself to the trouble when he might enlist the aid of so charming a helpmeet?"

Consuelo blushed, her hand shaking so much over the first spoonful that he was obliged to steady it with his own, but soon they were laughing together as they strove to coordinate their early attempts.

"I am still not clear about what happened, but Juan tells me that I owe my life as much to your initial presence of mind as to any skills he later employed," said Nick between mouthfuls. "You patched me up quite admirably, I believe."

She tilted the bowl and made a great business of collecting the last of the broth in the spoon, her head bent as she muttered that if she had not, those great boobies would undoubtedly have allowed him to bleed to death for want of a little common sense.

"Very likely." He stayed her busy hand, and as she

sat quite still he raised her chin with an insistent finger. "You are an extraordinary girl, do you know that? I make you my thanks."

He could not know how clamorously her heart was beating against her ribs as she schooled herself to meet his eyes with some degree of composure. No words would come, but he did not appear to expect any, for with a weary sigh he leaned back against his pillows.

"I am only sorry that I failed so abysmally in return to get you released from this place. I had hoped to talk some sense into that preposterous, amoral rogue, but he hasn't changed. That damaged foot may have slowed him down a trifle, but he's still obstinate, still ruthlessly committed to his lawless ways—and, like a child, taking refuge in temper when crossed!"

"But he can be kind, also," Consuelo said, still very conscious of her indebtedness to the man.

"Oh, he is! A veritable charmer, withal! And I'm bound to admit that there is no one I would liefer have at my back in a fix, but . . ." Nick moved his head on the pillow. "Anyhow, my words were to no avail, for he had already dispatched his demands to your father. So perhaps you will not be obliged to remain here too much longer." His smile had a certain wryness. "I doubt the conditions are to Lady Covington's liking!"

"No," she said, and added impulsively, "but I do not care how long I stay." Meeting his curious glance, she offered by way of explanation: "Did El Terremoto tell you that Don Miguel is already at the villa?"

"Oh, damn!" said Nick softly. "And I cannot help you. Well, it seems that Lord Linton will have to fight his own battle." Lost in the bitterness of his own feelings, it was some moments before he noticed her lack of response. "Consuelo?"

She said in a breathless little rush, "Lord Linton and I no longer wish to marry!" She laced her fingers together and stared down at them.

"I see," he said slowly. "Is this your decision—or his?" He held his own breath as he awaited her answer.

Nervously she slid from the bed, not wanting to betray herself to him. With her back to him she said very brightly. "It was by mutual agreement. I . . . we found that we did not . . . that is, our affections were not sufficiently engaged, and so . . ." *Ah, Dios*, she was making a dreadful mess of explaining.

"Consuelo?" Was there a different note in his voice, or was it simply that she so longed to hear it? "Come here, mi Consuelo . . ." This time there was no mistaking the tenderness. She turned slowly and found his eyes full of love.

He held out a hand in wry frustration. "Have pity, *mi queridísima!* There is no possible way I can come to you!"

She wanted to fly across the room and fling herself upon him, but, very conscious of his injury, she walked forward and put her hand into his. He drew her down onto the couch beside him until he was able to encircle her with his arm.

It was thus that El Terremoto found them presently, and with much gravity prophesied a return of his patient's fever. Nick told him amiably to "go to the devil," upon which the brigand chief brandished a razor. Consuelo stiffened instinctively and he, seeing this, laughed, his teeth very white.

"Have no fear, little one, I have come but to shave this precious captain of yours!" And indeed, Consuelo saw that Paco had followed him in, bearing a basin and towels. "A gentleman, you know, feels very much more the thing when he is washed and shaved."

"Yes, of course," she said, but showed little inclination to leave the safe haven of Nick's arm.

"You are naturally most welcome to remain," he continued with a wicked twinkle. "But I feel I should point out to you that we are also to strip Nicholas and wash him before putting him into clean linen!"

As she fled, suffused with blushing confusion, his uproarious laughter followed her down the stairs.

All was quietness below, and for this she was grateful. It was as though her whole life had been upturned at a stroke. She needed time to savor what had happened, to bring her teeming thoughts into some kind of order.

Surely her father could not deny Captain Bannion's suit? Or was she being precipitate? He had not mentioned marriage—or even that he loved her! But then, she reassured herself hastily, there had been no opportunity—and besides, one could tell. It was a feeling, here inside; she clasped her hands to her breast where the bubbles of happiness were welling up.

There was a disturbance at the door. One of the brigands came hurrying in, stopped short upon seeing her, cast a lowering glance about him and demanded to know the whereabouts of his chief. When told, he strode away, taking the stairs two at a time.

Consuelo shrugged and resumed her daydreaming undisturbed until she heard El Terremoto's uneven tread descending.

"Señorita?" There was an inflection in his voice, which, had she been attending, she might have recognized as pity. "Word has come from your father's house."

Her heart gave an involuntary shudder of dismay.

"He has paid? So soon? Oh, but we cannot possibly leave at this time! Captain Bannion is not ready to travel."

He limped across the room toward her and, taking her hand, led her to the nearby couch. "Come, we will sit here together and talk."

Now at last she heard the pity, and was gripped by a dreadful premonition. The blood drained from her face. "Tell me," she insisted.

He patted her hand. "The ransom is paid, yes— but not by your father. It is Don Miguel who writes with considerable urgency demanding your immediate release. I grieve to tell you, little one, that your father collapsed upon learning of your capture. Now, the don says, he lies mortally ill, and in his lucid moments asks constantly for you."

"He could be lying!" Consuelo cried out of desperation.

"No. It is true. My man learned it from one of the servants."

"I see. Then I must go." A kind of dull acceptance began to take over. It was foolish, after all, to hope that one could ever escape one's fate. She made no protest when Lady Covington came to sweep her off to make ready for the journey without permitting her first to see Captain Bannion.

"No time for that now, my love," said Verena firmly, urging her in the opposite direction.

"I have told Nicholas," El Terremoto assured her kindly. "He is much distressed to be so helpless, but is in no doubt that you must go."

In a bewilderingly short space of time during which she was not allowed a moment to herself to think, all was accomplished and they were crowding into the little turret room to bid Captain Bannion farewell.

There was an air of unreality about the occasion,

with Nick gritting his teeth against light-headedness and pain to tell Lady Covington stiffly that the *Spanish Lady* was at her disposal should she wish to return to England and that he would pen a brief note to Mr. Fletcher informing him of this.

But Verena had had enough of ships for the present and rather thought she might travel as far as Madrid to stay with friends for a while: "Though, naturally, I shall wish to see dear Consuelo safely disposed first!" She made a graceful gesture which set the twilled silk of her jade-green gown rippling. "Henry, of course, must do as he pleases."

Henry looked uncomfortable and muttered that he had not yet decided what his plans would be.

Consuelo said nothing. She had thought that perhaps it would be easier to say good-bye to Captain Bannion like this—in company. But it was impossible. She could only look at him as he expressed with a strange formality his regret that he could not go with her, his hope that he would be able to make the journey very soon and the added hope that she would find her father much improved.

His face, newly shaved, was pale and drawn and almost frighteningly grim. Any words she might have uttered were frozen in her throat, and the thought came illogically into her mind that this was what it must be like to die.

And then the agony was over and they were downstairs and ready to leave, Henry, dimly aware of her distress, supported her.

The carriage, said El Terremoto, would be awaiting them at the mouth of the pass. "From there, the journey is but a short one." He addressed himself with unfeigned gentleness to Consuelo. "May God go with you, little señorita. All will come well, have no fear; Nicholas is in excellent hands, and the moment he is fit to travel, I will bring him to you!"

It was as though his words released her from some spell that had held her impotent. She came alive; oblivious of Lady Covington's air of cold disapproval, she pulled herself from Henry's clasp and ran for the stairs, heedless of their protests.

Just inside the door she stopped. Nick lay back with his eyes closed and such acute misery etched in the pain-wracked lines of his face that she uttered a little cry of distress.

Nick thought for a moment that he had imagined the sound, but he opened his eyes and she was there. He uttered a faint sigh and held out his hand.

Consuelo rushed forward and flung herself down to be gathered against him.

"I won't go!" she gasped. *"Oh please*—say I need not go!"

"You must," he said, pushing back her bonnet to stroke her hair, kissing her lovely mouth with unbearable longing. "Oh, God, why must I be so helpless just when you need me!" He looked up and saw Henry standing in the doorway. There was a curious blindness in his eyes as he looked at the younger man and his voice grated, "Don't let them coerce her into anything, do you hear?"

Chapter 16

The cabriolet, drawn by a sturdy mule, came sedately down the Vitoria road as if in answer to the mournful summons of the tolling bell. It turned just beyond the church to make its way upward, winding between white walls from which the sun beat blindingly back.

Nick felt the clammy trickle of perspiration on his neck, induced by weakness as much as by the energy-sapping heat. He stared fixedly at Paco's back, hunched in disapproval, and willed himself to master the light-headedness that still, upon the least exertion, threatened to overwhelm him.

It was now three unbearably long days since he had received Henry Linton's letter, a letter penned in haste and delivered to him by way of Consuelo's maid Maria, who had entrusted it to the friend of a friend who knew one of the brigands. It had done nothing to reassure him.

Henry told how they had arrived at the Vasquez house to find the señor close to death and Don Miguel and his sister very much in control, and how the latter had taken charge of the shocked and unresisting Consuelo at once, barely allowing her time to bid Verena and himself good-bye. He and Lady Covington were accorded only the minimum of courtesy without a hint of hospitality.

"It was all deucedly awkward—chilling, you know," Henry's letter ran on. "The don and his sister spoke no English, and we had no more than a smattering of Spanish between us, but I had the strongest impression that he held us to blame for the whole business and couldn't wait to see the back of us. Even Verena's most haughty manner had little effect. The long and short of it is that we have been given the use of the señor's carriage, and Verena is now minded to travel to Paris of all places, and is adamant that I must accompany her.

"I swear that if there was the least chance that I might help Consuelo by remaining, I would do so, but I doubt that anyone can help her now, Bannion, even you. She is more closely imprisoned in that house than the most hopeless wretch in the Fleet, and with about as much chance of release. And even if she were not—I managed a word with Maria, who reckons that Consuelo has lost all her will to fight. . . ."

In consequence of this news, Nick had spent the past three days upon a rack of mental anguish while he willed his body to attempt the near impossible, and El Terremoto remonstrated with him for his foolishness.

"You are crazy, my friend! Of what use will you be to the little señorita if you insist upon trying your strength too soon? Are we not getting word every day of the good señor? As long as he clings to life, nothing can happen."

"And if he dies?" Nick's voice was hoarse. "I must see him before it is too late, and every day I delay the odds grow shorter!"

"You really believe that this swaggering hidalgo

would spirit the little one away with such unseemly haste? Would there not be talk?"

Nick shrugged. "Much he would care for that. With a fortune the size of Consuelo's almost within his grasp, my guess is that he'll seek to secure it with all speed."

The brigand flung out his arms. "The more you tell me, the more impossible do I find your expectation that you can remove the little one without force. Listen, my friend, you have but to say the word and I will have her away from that place in a trice!"

A faint answering smile lit Nick's eyes. "It may come to that yet. But we will try it my way first."

The late Señor Vasquez's residence lay behind intricately worked iron gates set into a high white wall. There was an uncomfortable delay before Nick was admitted into the courtyard, which did not auger well for his visit. Beyond the gates all seemed much as usual; palm trees provided welcome shade, and amid a bower of rich vines the gentle splashing of a fountain gave the illusion of coolness. But today there was tension where peace was wont to prevail.

The porter at the door recognized him and ushered him straightway into the room he remembered well, where the heavy lace curtains cast shimmering patterns across pale walls. He expressed his sorrow at the señor's passing, but though the servant looked close to tears, he would not be drawn to speak, and as he left the room Nick was more than ever conscious of an atmosphere about the place that was not due solely to the passing of a loved master.

He sank wearily into a chair and was forced to rise again almost immediately as the door opened behind him—and closed again.

The man who stood before him in deepest black

was short in stature, and when he moved, he strutted rather than walked, with a stiffness that suggested rigid corseting. The smooth, thin-lipped face gave nothing away.

Nick repeated his distress at the death of his old friend. It was coolly received by Don Miguel Alphonso de Aranches, who did not invite him to sit; instead he subjected him to a hard stare and, in a light but incisive voice, harangued him upon his incompetence in allowing his party to fall into the hands of brigands.

Nick kept his temper with an effort and allowed the don to finish.

"The shock of learning that his daughter was in the hands of such villainous men was more than the señor's delicate constitution could withstand. In the long run, I fear, it proved fatal."

"I am sorry." Nick's hands curled into angry fists until the nails bit deep, but still he would not be drawn. "I counted Señor Vasquez my friend and would have spared him had it been possible. However, wishing won't bring him back and it is Consuelo's well-being that now more deeply concerns me."

The thin lips pursed angrily. "You may safely leave Consuelo to me."

"Surely that is for her to decide. If you will be so good as to inform her that I am here, I think you will find her more than willing to see me."

Don Miguel was standing beside the wide mahogany desk where Señor Vasquez had conducted most of his business. He picked up the dagger with the jeweled hilt, which had been there for as long as Nick could remember, and tapped it lightly on the palm of his hand.

"I think you do not fully understand. Captain Bannion. Consuelo is no longer your concern, having been given solely into my charge. She is very young and has been guilty of much foolishness in the recent past. However, in these last distressing days she has been brought to recognize her own culpability in the matter of her father's last illness, and has learned, *gracias a Dios*, to be a dutiful daughter in all things. She was at the señor's side almost constantly at the end and her composure is consequently in a fragile state. I really cannot permit you to disrupt it." The slight inclination of his head indicated dismissal. "You may be sure that she is in good hands. My sister is her constant solace."

Nick grasped a chair back for support as anger, violent and uncontrollable, brought sudden dizziness washing over him, leaving him drained and shaking. He struggled to master it, cursing his weakness yet again. He remembered Henry's words: "Consuelo has lost all her will to fight. . . ." and apprehension hardened his resolve.

"You take too much upon yourself, señor. My obligation was to Consuelo's father, and I shall not consider it discharged until I hear from Consuelo's own lips that she is content. I refuse to leave until I have seen her."

"You are a very foolish man, Captain." Don Miguel's confidence seemed undiminished, though his hand shook slightly as he set down the dagger, and the light voice had grown a trifle shrill. "I could, of course, have you thrown out, but you would doubtless continue to delude yourself."

He strutted across the room to the door and flung it open. "Leo, you will inform Doña Isabella that she is to bring your mistress down to the study immediately."

As Nick waited he wondered at the ease with which the Don had assumed command. Señor Vasquez was hardly cold, yet already this man had taken complete control of his house, his servants and—or so it would seem—his daughter. His apprehension returned in full measure.

The door opened and Consuelo entered with an overpoweringly large older woman looming protectively at her shoulder. Both were in deepest black, and veiled. On Doña Isabella the effect was oppressive to the point of menace, but Consuelo appeared as a beautiful wraith, head bent in an attitude of submission. For an instant Nick was blinded by the red haze swimming before his eyes.

"Put back your veil, Consuelo. You have a visitor."

The don's voice was authoritative and she obeyed rather like a mechanical doll, lifting her head as she did so. A small indistinguishable sound escaped her and was swiftly bitten back.

Her face, exquisitely framed by the thrown-back mantilla, was quite bloodless, and those bright eyes, which had so often brimmed with merriment or flashed with occasional fury, were now black lackluster pools, devoid of expression—except for that one leaping second when they first met his.

"Are you all right, dearest?" he asked urgently, taking advantage of the English that the don and his sister did not understand.

She nodded, her mouth going wildly awry at the endearment. "And you?" she asked, low-voiced. "How pale you are. You should not . . ."

Impatiently, he dismissed her concern. "I am deeply sorry about your father."

Once more she nodded.

Frustration gripped him. Abandoning caution, he stepped forward to take her hands. Again he felt that involuntary response which leaped into life before it could be controlled. "Consuelo," he began forcefully, very much aware of the intimidating shadow of Doña

Isabella, and questioning at the back of his mind the curious staying gesture of Don Miguel when his sister would have intervened. Was he *that* sure of himself?

It would seem that he was. "I do feel, Captain Bannion, that you might accord us the politeness of conducting your conversation in Spanish." The light voice was almost bland.

Nick felt the trickle of perspiration cold on his back. He forced himself to continue. If he could only break down that unnatural composure, he could surely win Consuelo over, no matter what the hold they had on her. So let them hear what he had to say.

"Consuelo," he repeated, holding her hands very firmly and speaking slowly and distinctly. "I want you to come with me now, away from this place, back to the *Spanish Lady*. We will sail for England tonight and be married at the first possible moment."

There was an indignant hiss from Doña Isabella, but he ignored it, his whole concentration fixed on Consuelo, who shuddered, her eyes grown suddenly enormous.

"Ah no!" It was an agonized whisper. Her fingers gripped his painfully tight and she seemed to sway. But almost at once she recovered. "It is not possible," she said in a stifled voice.

"Anything is possible!" he insisted.

She shook her head with unbearable resignation. Looking up, Nick intercepted the gleam of triumph in the glance that passed between the Spaniard and his sister. Angrily he freed his hands and seized Consuelo by the shoulders.

"That will do, Captain. This affecting little scene has gone far enough." Don Miguel's voice flicked like a lash.

"No, by God! It has not!"

"Yes, by God, it has! You have had your answer. Now, you will oblige me by unhanding my wife!"

His wife! Nick's ears heard the words, heard the unmistakable ring of truth in them, but his mind totally rejected them. He still clung to Consuelo, feeling her despair, aware that if he released her he would fall, and marveling at her fortitude.

"The padre performed the ceremony at the señor's bedside shortly after midnight," the shrill voice continued inexorably. "It was the last wish of Consuelo's father. He died very soon after, content that his child was in safe hands."

"Safe!" The mist cleared from Nick's eyes. "Is that what you call it?" He summoned all his strength and shook Consuelo. "Listen to me, *querida*. A marriage like this, agreed to under duress, can be set aside. . . ."

"No." Her head moved warily. "I gave my father a solemn promise. . . ."

"For pity's sake, Consuelo! Don't be a fool! You can't throw away your whole life and hope of happiness because of some idiotic deathbed promise extracted under God knows what emotional pressures! It's—damn it, it's archaic!"

But he knew he had lost the argument, for though she flinched at his words, with her father still lying upstairs hardly cold, the events were too seared on her mind to be lightly put aside. And his resources of strength were exhausted, though a slow unremitting rage consumed him.

Beads of moisture stood out on his forehead as he released her and stepped back unsteadily. This almost proved to be her breaking point. With the Doña Isabella already urging her from the room, Consuelo could not take her eyes from his. She half put out a hand, her voice a stifled sob.

"Oh, but you look so ill! You should not have

come! Please, do not grieve for me . . . and . . . God go with you!" Her hand fell away and she turned and left him.

Don Miguel rang for the servant to show him out.

"Don't think this is the end of the matter." Nick ground the words out. "You may think you have been very clever, filling Consuelo's mind with a lot of religious hocus-pocus, but . . ."

"I have said not one word to influence her. Consuelo's own conscience . . ."

"Conscience be damned! Anyone but a fool can see that the poor girl is in an acute state of shock. But that won't last, and Consuelo has too much spirit to submit to anyone—least of all you, or that gorgon of a sister you keep as a jailer!"

"That is enough, Captain!" shrilled the Spaniard, all too aware of the servant standing by obsequiously but listening to every word. "You will leave now; and should you have any thoughts of returning, forget them. Señor Vasquez will be buried early tomorrow morning, and soon after that, we too shall leave. . . ."

"Unseemly haste, wouldn't you say?" Nick sneered. "What will Señor Vasquez's friends and neighbors think, do you suppose?"

"I trust they will extend a very natural sympathy when it is learned that the señor's daughter was so upset that I elected to remove her from the scene of her distress with all speed." His voice hardened. "Until then, this house will be well guarded. Go back to your ship, Captain Bannion, and forget that you ever knew Doña Consuelo."

Not a chance, thought Nick, his mind already grappling with ways and means.

Outside, Paco and the mule dozed in the welcome shade, but Paco, his senses finely tuned to the least sound, opened an eye to see Nick walk wearily and none too steadily from the door of the villa—alone.

He gave Nick a hand up and flicked the mule to set it in motion. "So, my friend, the little señorita stays, heh?"

"Not for much longer." Nick gave him the gist of what had transpired, his voice betraying him more than he guessed. "Look, you'd better take me to the ship. Then get back as quickly as you can and tell Juan what's happened. I must see him as soon as possible . . . in that coppice just beyond the Vasquez villa."

"You should take a rest, Señor Nick," Paco advised him dourly, without much hope of being heeded. "Already you have driven yourself beyond your strength."

Mr. Fletcher said much the same thing upon seeing him. He had received a full account from Lord Linton of all that had passed since the party left the ship, but this was the first time he had actually seen Nick, and he was deeply disturbed by his pallor, to say nothing of the absentminded way he occasionally pressed a hand to his side.

He had no hesitation in expressing his opinion most forcibly upon learning of Nick's latest escapade. "If you go on at this rate, I won't be responsible for you!"

"How can I rest?" Nick flung the words at him savagely. "I tell you, Bob, there was something downright frightening about that girl's composure! As though she was on the edge of hell with no means of retreat! I simply have to get her away from that house before morning."

"Well, you can't do anything until this brigand fellow turns up," said Bob Fletcher reasonably. "So why not snatch a couple of hours sleep meanwhile?

And a good stiff tot of rum wouldn't come amiss either. You'll be a deal more use to the señorita when the time comes."

Nick, unable any longer to ignore the nagging pain in his side, acknowledged the sense in Bob's reasoning and succumbed to his unutterable weariness, having first extracted a promise that he would be awakened the moment El Terremoto sent word.

Chapter 17

Maria was surprised when Consuelo came back so quickly from seeing Captain Bannion, looking more than ever like a little ghost. It had seemed like an answer to a prayer when Maria learned of the captain's arrival; she wasn't quite sure what she had expected of him; perhaps she was hoping for a miracle. And after what she had just heard down in the kitchens, that was just about what it was going to need.

Downright wicked, it was! There was no other way to describe what had gone on under this roof in the last few days, and if she couldn't talk some sense into her young mistress and get her away to safety before morning, then it was all up for her.

Maria waited, fuming with impatience, while that old witch Doña Isabella prated on about duty, though she might have saved her breath, for it was clear that the señorita—Maria refused to think of her as otherwise—wasn't listening. At last the older woman left, and Consuelo walked across to the window and stared blindly out.

"Señorita, I must talk with you!" Maria put her plump, homely face very close to her mistress's and implored her to listen. It was like addressing a block of wood. Finally, in sheer desperation, she took her by the shoulders, much as Nick had done earlier, and shook her, though not as gently.

"Very well!" she cried, close to tears. "If you wish to spend the rest of your life locked away in a nunnery, then do not attend me! I am sure I don't know why I should worry myself into such a state if you will not even trouble to listen!"

At first there was no reaction to her plea; then, very slowly, Consuelo turned her head. "What did you say?"

"Ah, *gracias a Dios!*" sobbed the maid. "At last! Señorita, you must listen to me! When you were called away just now, I slipped down to the kitchen, and Beatrice, Doña Isabella's woman was there. She is as sour-faced as her mistress, and we fell to quarreling. In the course of exchanging insults, she let fall that I should make the most of the time left to me as I would very soon be out of a job. . . ."

Consuelo was trying very hard to take in what her maid was saying, but all that she could think of was her beloved captain looking so pale and so hurt by her seeming rejection of him. It was as though she had been in a trance, her brain numbed by too many emotional shocks coming one upon the other.

Now, suddenly, reality was being forced in upon her—by Nick's visit, and now by Maria's air of urgency. It was a little like having mental pins and needles; her heart began to thud uncomfortably, and its increasing clamor brought with it all the sensations of pain and guilt and heartbreak that she had blotted out.

"Oh, Maria! I am sorry that I am being so stupid!" She swung around, unable any longer to remain still. "You spoke of a nunnery?"

Maria watched her pacing the room, her mantilla cast aside, one hand riffling through her hair—with every moment that passed becoming more her old self. The maid bit her lip, suddenly diffident about speaking with such frankness. Yet if she did not . . .

"Forgive me, señorita!" she blurted out at last. "It is not for me to know, let alone speak of such matters, but it is a thing you should know . . . and with the time so short, there is no one else to tell you. . . ."

"Yes, yes . . . do get on!" Consuelo rounded on her with so much of her old spirit that Maria felt much more at ease.

"Well, it seems that Beatrice overheard a conversation between her mistress and Don Miguel . . . which is a thing that I entirely believe, for she is just the kind of person who would creep about listening at doors."

"Maria!"

"Yes . . . yes, of course, señorita. Forgive me. I cannot vouch for exactly what was said, you understand, but according to Beatrice, Don Miguel was furious when you did not return home in good time for your wedding, and even more furious when he discovered the cause! It is his pride, of course; to be spurned for a younger man is not pleasant. After the kidnap Doña Isabella was all for abandoning you to your fate, but when El Terremoto's ransom note came . . . well, Don Miguel still had an eye to your fortune . . . forgive my presumption, señorita . . ."

"Yes, yes!"

She saw that Consuelo had halted in her pacing and that she now had her full attention. The words came rushing out.

"And when your father, God rest him, collapsed, Don Miguel saw a way to be revenged upon you for your slight to his pride *and* gain control of your inheritance. Thus your travesty of a marriage. It would not be difficult to put the idea into the señor's head that your future would be thus secured. . . ." Disgust was apparent in Maria's voice. "When the lawyers have arranged matters and all is signed and sealed, he means to let it be known that the shock of your father's death turned your brain and that he has no choice, for your own peace of mind, you understand, but to deliver you into the safekeeping of some suitable convent."

"But that is monstrous!" Consuelo cried. "He will not be able to carry it through! There are too many people here who know that I am not mad!"

"Certainly. Which is why Don Miguel means to hurry the burial through and take you south at once—tomorrow. Beatrice was very sure of herself. She said that it is already being arranged with the superior of a convent in Cordoba that you are to be admitted there for a complete rest almost immediately."

"*Dios!* Then there is not a moment to be lost! Oh, why did I send Nicholas away?"

Galvanized into action, Consuelo was already tugging at the buttons of her dress. Maria hurried to help her. The unconscious familiarity of her reference to the captain had not gone unnoticed and, taken with something Lord Linton had said before he left, showed the maid quite clearly where her young mistress's heart now lay.

"Can we not get a message to the good captain?" she asked hopefully.

"Yes, of course." Consuelo half dressed, rushed to the desk, to write one. "Ah, but no!" She looked up in dismay. "He looked so ill! It would be impossible to permit him to endanger himself." Her hand still hovered over the paper. "If only it were possible to call upon El Terremoto . . ."

"The brigand?"

"But certainly. Who better, after all, to kidnap one

than a brigand? He accomplished it very successfully once; why should he not do it again?"

Consuelo's sudden grin did more than anything to assure Maria that her mistress was well on the way to recovery. From the little she had heard, the episode in the mountains had sounded vastly romantic, and she was much grieved not to have shared it.

She said almost coquettishly, "There is a way, señorita. Rafael, who is paying me court, has a friend, and *he* knows well how to make contact with the brigands."

"But that is splendid. See, I will write him a note and your Raphael must get it to him very quickly." A frown creased Consuelo's brow, but already the prospect of intrigue was putting the color back into her cheeks. "You will tell them downstairs that I am sleeping from exhaustion, and then you must seize your chance to slip out."

For an instant her ebullience wavered. "What I am doing is not so very wrong, do you think?"

Nick came out of a heavy sleep filled with dreams of searching endlessly for Consuelo, with Don Miguel blocking his path at every turn.

He sat up abruptly, aware instantly from the sun's angle that he had slept far too long. He shook his head and the cabin settled round him. Cursing heartily, he stopped only to douse his head in the bowl of water on the stand before hurrying, half stumbling up on deck.

The late-afternoon sun was bouncing back with eye-aching ferocity from the white walls along the quayside. Nick called for Mr. Fletcher, who came running almost at once.

"Bob, you crass, misguided dunderhead! Why didn't you wake me before now? Don't you realize that I've lost precious hours? And where the devil is Juan? Paco should have been back with him long before now!"

"If you will only calm down for a moment . . ." Bob Fletcher began wryly, and stopped as a carriage came clattering along the quay. Nick's head lifted hopefully as it stopped, though reason told him that it was too elegant a vehicle by far for El Terremoto.

A lackey sprang down to open the door and let down the steps for Don Miguel Alphonso de Aranches to descend. He strutted across the quay, looking neither to right nor left, his black coat fitting his well-corseted torso like a second skin, the ruffles of lace at the cuff its only relief. At his back, dwarfing him, came two grim-faced young argonauts.

Nick watched grimly as the party came aboard, his greeting terse as he bade the don state his business, then get off his ship.

Fury leaped into the Spaniard's eyes, but it was quickly controlled. "My business, Captain, concerns my wife, who disappeared from her bedchamber some time this afternoon when she was supposed to be resting."

Surprise, uncertainty, followed by the swift joy of knowing that Consuelo was free, though he knew not how, flooded through Nick in quick succession. He was hard pressed to keep his feelings from showing as he said, "Really? How very sensible of her."

"She did not accomplish her departure unaided." The light voice was beginning to take on its shrill note. "Several of my servants were rendered senseless and tied up in a particularly vicious way!"

Nick was beginning to understand. "So? Why do you come to me?"

"*Caramba*! Do you take me for a fool?"

"What I take you for is hardly pertinent at this

moment," Nick drawled provocatively and had the satisfaction of making Don Miguel go crimson with anger.

"Can you deny that my wife is on this ship?" he squeaked.

Nick glanced surreptitiously at Bob Fletcher, whose face wore so bland an expression that one would swear he was innocent of all knowledge concerning Consuelo's whereabouts, but several of the crew were grinning behind their hands.

"I appreciate your predicament, Don Miguel, but it is not within my power to help you." With a scrupulous regard for the truth he added, "I have not laid eyes on Consuelo since this morning."

The Spaniard was tenacious to the last. "Then you can have no possible objection to my men making a search of your ship, lest she might perhaps have slipped aboard unseen?" he said with heavy sarcasm.

But Nick was suddenly tired of playing verbal games. He had far more pressing matters on his mind. So: "Oh, but I do object," he said softly, stepping forward in so menacing a fashion that Don Miguel was obliged to retreat a pace. "I find every moment of your continuing presence aboard the *Spanish Lady* loathsome in the extreme—so much so, in fact, that if you do not leave immediately I shall take steps to have you removed." Behind him he heard the eager shuffling of feet. "I hope I make myself plain?"

It was probable that no one had ever spoken to the pompous hidalgo in quite that way before. His eyes bulged with repressed fury, but a need to retain what dignity was left to him in the presence of his two expressionless lackeys made him draw himself up stiffly. He executed a formal bow and turned to leave.

At the last, however, spite overruled prudence. "You are welcome to her!" He spat the words out. "Nevertheless, she is still my wife. . . ."

"In name only," Nick cut in, hoping to God that he was right.

"That you will have to prove. I will fight any attempt to have the marriage annulled, and since I am not without influence in high places, you are like to find yourself saddled with a destitute." Triumph made him careless. "She could always live as a *puta*—in view of her recent exploits, the role should become her well!"

Nick's fist smashed into the smug face and the don sprawled senseless across the deck. The two lackeys moved menacingly forward and then thought better of taking on the whole crew.

Nick waited impassively until Don Miguel stirred, groaned and finally opened his eyes. He stared vacuously for a moment and then focused, found Nick's face and, as recollection dawned, burned red with rage. He moved and groaned again as his two lackeys rushed forward to lift him to his feet.

"Get him off my ship," Nick said. "But before you go, Don Miguel, hear this. I, too, am not without influence. My mother was a Carvalhos." He saw the Spaniard's start of surprise. "Quite so. Her elder brother, in case you are unaware of it, is at present Bishop of Tortosa, a man highly thought of in Rome. It is rumored that any day now he will be named a cardinal. I think we may be sure that such a man will be listened to above any other, and that with him to plead her case, Consuelo will obtain her annulment without any trouble whatever," Nick concluded, recklessly committing his unwitting uncle to their cause. He paused to let the information sink in before saying coldly, "That is all. Good-bye, Don Miguel."

He stood impassively until the party was ashore and driving away from the quay. Then, without looking around and with the tautness in his voice betraying an unbearable anxiety: "So . . . where exactly have you got Consuelo stowed?" Bob Fletcher chuckled, and Nick let go his breath, feeling that a weight had been lifted from him. "So I guessed right. Thank God!"

"She is in my cabin," Mr. Fletcher replied, "with Batty for company. Your brigand friend brought her on board about an hour since with her maid. She refused to allow me to waken you."

But he was talking to the air. Nick was already halfway down the companionway. At the cabin door he was obliged to pause—to steady his thudding heart and draw breath before flinging it open.

Two boyish figures sat side by side; two cropped heads bent in absorption over a game of cards laid out on the bunk between them. Both looked up— Batty with an ear-splitting grin as Consuelo sprang to her feet, scattering cards everywhere. She stood, her eyes questioning as they devoured his face. Then he opened his arms, and as if released by a spring, she rushed forward to be received in a crushing embrace. And promptly burst into tears.

"That's great," said Batty approvingly, but they didn't hear him. Neither did they notice as he sidled past them and out of the door, closing it softly behind him.

Consuelo's arms were clasped tightly about Nick's neck as though she would never let him go. "I am being very silly, I know," she sobbed joyfully through her tears. "But I had thought that I would never see you again! Everything has been so truly awful!"

"Truly awful," he agreed with feeling, remembering how she had been so short a time ago. But the tone of his voice recalled her suddenly to the fact that he was still far from well and should not be standing.

Nick assured her that he was improving by the minute, but to please her he sat on Bob Fletcher's bunk and pulled her onto his knee.

"Oh, but your poor wound!" she exclaimed.

"The devil take my wound! It is fast becoming a bore." He drew her close. "I am much more interested in you!" He plucked teasingly at her breeches. "I didn't realise you still had these."

"Neither did I," she confessed, blushing a little, "but Maria discovered them among my things and they seemed exactly right for escaping!" She settled blissfully into his shoulder and told him all that had happened, of Don Miguel's perfidy.

"One would not believe that such wickedness was possible!" she said, and in a more subdued voice: "I slipped into my father's room before I left and explained to him why I must break my vows and go. Somehow, he looked a little less severe in death . . . I think perhaps he will understand and forgive me. . . ."

Nick tightened his hold about her and said firmly that he was sure of it. She sighed her relief and continued with her story.

"I had written a message for El Terremoto which Maria was to have delivered to him, but it was not necessary, for he had followed you down from the mountains and was already waiting to rescue me! Wasn't that clever of him?" Her enthusiasm bubbled over. "His men knocked out Don Miguel's guards and then one of them climbed up to my window and helped us to tie the sheets together so that we could climb down! It was the greatest adventure!"

Nick laughed, overjoyed to have her restored to herself once more.

"El Terremoto considered it better not to involve you, *mi queridísimo* . . . because of your condition. You do not mind?" she asked anxiously. "Naturally, I would much prefer to have been rescued by you, but I am here now and we will never be separated again!" When he did not immediately agree, she looked up at him in sudden fear. "Will we? Don Miguel cannot make me return to him. I would kill myself. . . ."

"As if I would permit it! Hush now!" Nick kissed her upturned mouth with sudden urgency.

It was several minutes before any coherent conversation was resumed. Then Nick said, striving to be practical, "But the marriage must be annulled and your inheritance restored to you. It is but a formality, but it will take time."

"I don't care," she said blithely. "Until then, I can come with you on your voyages."

"No, you can't." He saw the stubborn tilt of her chin that he remembered from past encounters and said sternly, "What good will it do your cause, do you suppose, if it is learned that you are gallivanting around the world with me like some feckless jade?"

"I do not care what anyone thinks! Don Miguel may have my fortune for what good it may do him, and as for marriage—I do not care about that either, so long as I can be with you."

Nick's heart melted with love for her, but as the tears sprang to her eyes, he forced himself to remain firm.

"Well, I care a great deal, Consuelo; not about your fortune, though it would grieve me to see it go to such a villain, but"—he fell to coaxing—"oh come, *querida*, you surely do not wish our children to be bastards?"

Her mouth remained unyielding for a moment more, then it quivered and she giggled. "I had not thought!" And then, as she realized what he was asking of her: "But what is to become of me in the meantime?" she wailed.

Nick laughed softly and drew her close once more. "I wondered whether you might like to go and stay with Madame Garrishe for a little while? I'm sure she would be overjoyed to have you."

"Oh yes, I should enjoy that very much . . . as long as it is for a little while only," she amended anxiously.

"I swear it, sweetheart. One thing only . . ." He looked down at her, making his voice deliberately casual. "Don Miguel . . . he didn't . . . come near you? After the ceremony, I mean?"

"Certainly not," she said indignantly. "Even Don Miguel would not attempt *that* with my father on his deathbed—and our good padre so obviously disapproving of his unseemly haste in pushing through with the ceremony at such a moment!"

So the padre would be sympathetic? Nick's spirits lifted.

"And in any case," Consuelo added gleefully, "Maria locked the door of my bedchamber and vowed that he would enter only over her dead body!"

With the maid's corroboration to remove any lingering doubt, Don Miguel would be a fool to oppose the annulment.

"It is but a formality, then," Nick told her and, finding the closeness of her mouth irresistible, put the trouble from his mind and claimed her lips once more, meeting with so passionate a response that time ceased to have any meaning. Only very gradually did he become aware that the ship was moving beneath them.

He stirred and murmured against her ear, "It would seem that Mr. Fletcher, sensible of my preoccupation with more important matters, has anticipated my instructions. Shall we go up on deck, my dear love, and bid farewell to Spain?"

Later, Consuelo leaned against the rail with Nick's arm safely about her, and felt only the smallest pang as the shoreline receded.

"Oh see!" she cried, pointing eagerly toward the path leading to the mountains where several figures were clearly visible. As they watched, the leader, perched incongruously astride a mule with his long legs dangling, lifted an arm in salute. They waved back.

"I have just thought, *amigo*," said Consuelo, raising her head from his shoulder to smile provocatively up at him through her lashes. "I suppose one might say that we are eloping. And this time there will be no 'wicked captain' to prevent us."

About the Author

Sheila Walsh lives with her husband in South-port, Lancashire, England, and is the mother of two daughters. She began to think seriously about writing when a local writers' club was formed. After experimenting with short stories and plays, she completed her first Regency novel, *The Golden Songbird*, which subsequently won her an award presented by the Romantic Novelists' Association in 1974. This title, as well as her other Regencies—*Madalena, The Sergeant Major's Daughter, Lord Gilmore's Bride, The Incomparable Miss Brady, The Rose Domino*, and *A Highly Respectable Marriage*—are available in Signet editions.